THE CLOSETS OF TIME

EDITED BY RICHARD TRUHLAR
& BEVERLEY DAURIO

THE CLOSETS OF TIME

A NEW FICTION ANTHOLOGY

THE
MERCURY
PRESS

The publisher gratefully acknowledges the financial assistance of the Canada Council for the Arts, the Ontario Arts Council, the Ontario Media Development Corporation, and the Ontario Book Publishing Tax Credit Program. The publisher further acknowledges the financial support of the Government of Canada through the Department of Canadian Heritage's Book Publishing Industry Development Program (BPIDP) for our publishing activities.

Canada Council for the Arts   Conseil des Arts du Canada

ONTARIO ARTS COUNCIL
CONSEIL DES ARTS DE L'ONTARIO

Ontario
Ontario Media Development Corporation
Société de développement de l'industrie des médias de l'Ontario

Canada

Editors: Richard Truhlar & Beverley Daurio
Cover design: Gordon Robertson
Text design: Beverley Daurio

Printed and bound in Canada
Printed on acid-free paper

1 2 3 4 5   11 10 09 08 07

Library and Archives Canada Cataloguing in Publication

    The closets of time / Beverley Daurio, Richard Truhlar, [editors].
  ISBN 978-1-55128-133-9
    I. Daurio, Beverley, 1953- II. Truhlar, Richard, 1950-
  PS8323.D74C55 2007   C814'.54   C2007-904906-0

The Mercury Press
Box 672, Station P, Toronto, Ontario Canada M5S 2Y4
www.themercurypress.ca

CONTENTS

THE CLOSETS OF TIME

LANCE OLSEN

WHAT YOU SEE BEFORE YOU. Ladies and Gentlemen, is a closet composed of smaller closets, a cabinet composed of thirteen miniature doors. Behind each resides a compartment lodging a small remarkable portion of The Man with Borrowed Organs. The portions have come to us from as far away as Machu Picchu and Borneo, Burma and Bhutan. The Man himself, first assembled in 1816, sleeps behind this second door, here, which remains locked. You will not observe him today. He is assembled once every thirty years, and then only for the precise interval of three minutes and thirty-three seconds for reasons that, I believe, will become clear shortly.

Let me invite you to feast your eyes on the man divided...

1. FINGERNAILS, TOENAILS, HAIR

These items, said to have been stolen by a Norwegian explorer in 1824 from a glass case in a Nepalese monastery near Pokhara, were originally removed from the corpse of an angel. Once upon a time, as you may recall, we believed such creatures beautiful pale beings with white swan wings. It was only with this case that we discovered they were in fact ugly dwarfish beasts covered with coarse orange hair. Their wings resemble those, not of swans, but bats, are slightly larger than a human palm, and serve no purpose save dreaming of heaven, a place from which some, without warning, have been excluded. Cornered, an earthbound angel will curl into a ball so tiny it can actually slip between cracks in time, thereby creating the impression of invisibility. Monks caught this individual by staking a naked weeping boy bathed in red wine in the middle of an opening in the forest at night. The prey became drunk on the boy's carcass. Two months later, it expired of loneliness and temporal awareness in a rusty cage usually reserved for fattening hogs.

Wearing these fingernails, toenails, and hair, The Man with Borrowed Organs learns every moment that human beings continually grow, but always in ultimately useless ways.

2. LIPS

Excised from a Burmese princess on her thirteenth birthday in 1753 by her father, who frowned upon the idea of her kissing boys, these dry thin brown virgin folds are meant to remind The Man with Borrowed Organs what one can no longer say.

3. TEETH

Each of these, in various stages of decay, was taken from the mouth of a falsely accused murderer on the morning he met his hangman, strangler, swordsman, firing squad, horde of stoners, blank-faced flunky who threw the switch on the electric chair or dropped crystals of sodium cyanide into the pail of sulfuric acid or let the guillotine's blade plummet, sad-faced doctor who lifted the shiny syringe.

Together, these teeth chew the same memories over and over again, until they are pulpy as pap.

4. STOMACH

At first you might mistake this organ for a huge dark lilac bagpipe. It once belonged to the legendary giant Goliath who, as you well know, fell by the hand of David of the Israelites in the Valley of Elah. When David confronted him, carrying only a sling and sack filled with five smooth stones he'd collected from a nearby stream, Goliath mocked the boy. When David paid Goliath's words no heed, Goliath cursed him by all the names of the Philistine gods and lumbered at him, arms raised above his head, slaughter in his fierce eyes. Thinking quickly, David drew a stone from his bag and slung it, shattering the giant's temple. Goliath pitched forward onto the sand. The Holy Book claims David next beheaded his nemesis with a sword, yet the truth is the boy used that sword to gut the giant while he lay dazed and writhing before him. Done, David played upon Goliath's enormous stomach in front of Saul like a horrible wind instrument.

Here the memories the teeth have chewed mix in a broth of nostalgia. Some of the recollections there are real. Some are imaginary. With some, it is impossible to tell.

5. EYES

The brown one was picked up in fairly bad shape by a peasant along a dirt road running through Nagasaki on the evening of August 9th, 1945, a Thursday, and sold several weeks later to a U.S. Army physician, who, as a teenager, worked one summer preventing people from leaping off the observation deck at the edge of Niagara Falls. The green one belonged to a twenty-two-year-old girl whom a Pakistani tribal council ordered gang-raped on June 22nd, 2002, a Saturday, in order to punish her family after her eleven-year-old brother was seen walking with a girl from a higher-class tribe. The second eye was sold directly to us by a British ophthalmologist in Lahore, to replace our blue one of unknown origin, which had gone blind over time as a result, we surmise, of having seen too much.

By slipping these eyes into his empty sockets, The Man with Borrowed Organs is able to recall, each second he is awake, who we are not and can never be.

6. EARS

The unfortunate who originally possessed these could not hear. He passed his life as an uncelebrated musician in a sanatorium in Salzburg during the early years of the twentieth century. To this day, no one has been able to make heads or tails out of his compositions, although for a short time they drew the intense attention of Arnold Schoenberg. Like The Man with Borrowed Organs, we surmise this unfortunate lived in a land of cacophony others could not apprehend.

These knotty flaps of cartilage allow The Man with Borrowed Organs to bear in mind that every word we speak falls, at the end of the day, on deaf ears.

7. LUNGS

The lungs house hope.

As you can see, they are extremely small.

8. SKIN

You may have heard our skin is our largest organ. For the average adult, it boasts a surface area of two square metres and accounts for fifteen percent of body weight. An inch of it generally contains six-hundred-and-fifty sweat glands, twenty blood vessels, sixty-thousand pigment-producing melanocytes, and more than a thousand nerve endings. However, none of these facts holds true for this specimen. It was quilted from 1837 to 1842 out of the hide of thirty-three newborn albino females by an eighty-year-old woman who lived in a cave in northern India, and is so thin you can actually see the other organs of the body functioning beneath it, as in some species of transparent fish. It forms a suit slightly too small for The Man with Borrowed Organs, regrettably making it impossible for him to bend his arms and legs, or engage in such common activities as sitting, bowing, or genu-flecting, thereby edifying him on a constant basis about how each of us is imprisoned within himself while at the same time open to public scrutiny of the most severe kind.

9. HEART

The very presence of the lungs and skin dictates the necessity for an organ that produces emptiness, and, hence, the heart.

10. APPENDIX

This five-inch-long blind-ended tube the colour of Thousand Islands dressing that branches off from the intestinal pouch called the cecum has a two-fold purpose for The Man with Borrowed Organs. First, it helps define the notion of uncertainty for him. Thus it is considered the most philosophical organ. Second, it lets him know that whatever we do, however much we accomplish in the course of our lives, wherever we might travel, whoever we might meet, we will always have been more important at some point in the past.

11. TESTICLES

Removed from the body of a dreaming Amauta, or Incan wise man, hunted down and rendered unconscious by the Spanish conquistador Francisco Pizarro in 1533 at the advice of his trusted chroniclers, and passed along through the generations in a matriarchal line until coming to our attention by means of a museum curator (whose name, unfortunately, has since been lost to history) in Lima in 1952, these testicles, once kept on a plush pad of red velvet in an elaborate gold-topped glass container reminiscent of a philatory, as with them all, are where stories are created.

12. INTESTINES

Perhaps the most misunderstood organ, the intestines are usually thought to be that part of the digestive system responsible for breaking down and absorbing food. No definition could be more inadequate. As The Man with Borrowed Organs appears to know well, it also marks the place in the human anatomy (for other animals it is, naturally, different) where the testicles write their tales in runic-like scars. Depending on one's religious views, those tales form lists either of a person's successes or failures. Sadly, however, those scars evaporate upon contact with air, while being invisible to x-ray, computer tomography, and other similar methods of medical imaging, and so must, unfortunately, always remain a mystery.

That is why among some specialists this organ is also referred to as the Calendar of Regrets.

13. GOD

As you can see, there is nothing behind this door except a vacant compartment. Although there is a plethora of theories, no one has been capable of grasping with any certitude where this organ might reside, where it came from and how it developed, or what, precisely, it does. Conflicts have been waged across the world and through time in the belief that destroying one's enemy proves one's own assertions about this item true. Many people believe it exists before us, right here, but is undetectable except for its effects. Some believe it is simply one more product of the genitals. Others maintain it could only be dreamed by a heart of emptiness.

Whatever the case may be, lately we have been prone to exclude it when assembling The Man with Borrowed Organs, since it frequently leads him to experience, from what we can infer through his gestures, unmitigated fright, excruciating guilt, and brief instances of a false sense of security and hope, followed by crushing misery.

LESLEY McALLISTER

1-2-3-*

One-two-threeeee, one-two-threeeee, falling in love with you was easy for meeee, easy for meeee...

My sanitized fingers tap in the Riverside entry code, the automatic door swings open and I step into my mother's four-storey world of durable carpeting, soft music and chicken-noodle soup.

It's so eeeasy, it's so eeeasy, like taking can-dy from a ba-by.

It doesn't look like much of a security system, especially since the code is posted on the wall above the keypad. But it serves its purpose, getting people in and out and keeping residents like my mother tucked safely inside.

My mother is still able to read. She reads signs out loud all the time in a sweet falsetto belonging to someone else: *"Welcome to Riverside Manor"... "Today's*

Activities"… "All Staff Must Sign in with Shift Supervisor."
But she can't make the connection between 1-2-3 and
the keypad. She bangs away on it like she's eight years old
again and struggling with the piano, and gets angry when
nothing happens. Even if she figured out how to work it,
it wouldn't make any difference. Like all the residents on
the second floor, she wears a plastic monitoring bracelet
that overrides the system and locks the doors if she gets
within a few feet of them.

At first I was really anxious about visiting and would
get panic attacks on the walk over. The pavement would
roll under my feet and I'd think I was going to faint. And
when, the odd time, I couldn't get the doors to open, I'd
imagine the worst. But then one day something amazing
happened. I took a deep breath and stepped through the
glass doors into the overheated lobby, signed the visitors'
log as usual and—Hey, presto!—felt the anxiety slide off
my shoulders along with my heavy winter coat.

I visit as often as I can and spend a lot of time walking around and around the halls with my mother, smiling at the other lost souls and wondering what it is about
this place that makes me forget to be anxious. When my
mother first moved in, she thought we were on a holi-
day cruise and kept asking when we were going to land
back home.

On busy days I help at bingo, pointing out the numbers to players who don't see too well and adding a few
dollars to what my mother's friend Jean calls the "potty."

And we always turn up for karaoke Mondays. That's where we met Marv from the third floor. Sitting in front of the karaoke machine, eyes squeezed shut, belting out "What Kind of Fool Am I?" a la Frank Sinatra. My mother's crazy about Sinatra and she adores Marv, too, even though his singing makes her cry. Mr. Marvel, she calls him. Sometimes she introduces him to me as "my son," even though he doesn't look anything like my brother.

Most visits with my mother end up with us sitting by the window in the lounge. The conversation goes something like this: Me—"Look how blue the sky is today." Mom—"I like that car." Me—"Look, here comes someone walking a dog." Mom—"That's a nice car." Sometimes she gets the dogs and the cars mixed up and barks when a car pulls into the parking lot.

It's hard to know what to do with her to pass the time. Last week we had to slink out of the Dog Show after she rescued the little shivering poodle from its trainer and commanded it to "Bite him!"

This afternoon, though, she's on cloud nine. The home has organized an April Fool's Day Talent Show and Mr. Marvel's Marvellous Magic Show is the main act. There's still half an hour to go, but the more mobile residents are already streaming in, scuffing along in crêpe-soled bootie slippers, leaning on walkers or navigating electric scooters between rows of chairs.

When I cross the lobby on the way up to my mother's room, I can see Marv setting up. He's bebopping around in his wheelchair, humming some dance tune, spreading a midnight blue cloth over the bingo table and lining up his props. "What's goin' on?" he calls over and shoots me a big stage wink.

Marv spends a lot of time with my mother when I'm not here. He told me they sit together in her room, eating jelly babies and turning the pages of the Memory Book I made for her. His favourite photograph is the one of my mother, wrapped in a tartan trenchcoat, pushing me in my pram down Sauchiehall Street beaming with pride. "Is that me?" she asks him every time. My mother says Marv told her he's a miracle man, like Jesus.

When she first met Marv, my mother looked him up and down and said, "What are you doing in this place?"

"This poor heart of mine's got a big hole in it," he said.

"Well, I've got one in my poor head," my mother answered and they both laughed their heads off.

That was two years ago. It's been a while since my mother laughed like that. More and more these days her eyes are blank, like someone reached inside her head, pulled a master switch and turned off all the lights. Today she's got her cardigan on inside out so her cloth nametag is showing, and she's put her squashy beige slippers on the wrong feet. The stretched-out bit from her bunion is flopping around beside her little toe like a rabbit's ear. In the elevator going down, she holds my hand as tightly as a child in a busy shopping centre.

Every time I see Marv he looks natty and he always smells good, too. Today he's wearing a white satin jacket and a sky blue polka-dot shirt, his gray braids springing out from under a black top hat. The heavenly scent of patchouli wafts up from the blanket covering his legs. Tomorrow is Marv's birthday and for a gift he asked me to be his magician's assistant for his final trick. He's promised me he'll give up all his secrets after the show.

Whenever I ask him how he's doing, Marv always answers, "Rockin'." But I heard through the staff grapevine that he hasn't been eating well lately. And there's a droop to his shoulders I hadn't noticed before.

But the instant his wheels touch the stage, it's like someone pumped him full of helium.

"Has anyone here ever heard of the word 'Abracadabra'?" he bellows, raising his magic wand and looking around the room. A few people put up their hands. "Not many people know it, but Abracadabra is a magic word for finding things. I'll show you what I mean."

Marv steers over to Anna from the fourth floor and asks her to fold back his cuffs. "*I play my game of fantasy...*" he sings. "*I pretend that I'm not in reality.*" He spins around and holds his hands out, palms up, so we can see that they're empty. They're trembling just a little.

"One for my baby..." he says, passing his hand behind Anna's balding head and pulling a quarter out of her ear. "... and one more for the road." He reaches up and —

"Abracadrabra!" — pulls a loonie from thin air. Anna titters and holds up the coins. The spectators in the front row Ooh! and Aah!

"Can I get a witness for my next magic feat?" Marv asks. He pulls a pair of pink-framed X-ray glasses out of his pocket and slips them on. "Any poker players in the audience?"

Jean-Guy from the first floor puts up his hand and scoots to the stage. Marv asks him to shuffle a deck of playing cards, which he manages with only a few spills. "Now look at the card at the bottom of the deck... but don't tell me what it is!"

Jean-Guy scrunches up his face in concentration, then following Marv's instructions he slides the cards into their box and hands it back. Holding the deck up in front of him, Marv waves his magic wand over it.

"I want you all to say the magic words with me— Hocus pocus!"

"Hocus pocus!" we repeat.

"Is your card..." Marv pauses and rubs his forehead, "the... King of... Hearts?"

"I'll be doggone," says Jean-Guy. "How'd you do that?"

"Ah, we magicians can't give away our secrets. But I will tell you a secret about myself," Marv answers, picking up a cardboard shoebox and showing us that it's empty. "I used to love shoes. I had a different pair of shoes for every outfit—and I had lots of outfits."

He returns the box to the table and shows us both sides of the lid. "Man, I was trouble. That's what my daddy always told me." Then he puts the lid on the shoebox and covers it with a white handkerchief. He picks the box up and spins it once, twice—"Let's see if we can find me some dancing shoes"—three times.

"Hocus pocus!" we shout as Marv lifts the lid off with a flourish.

He reaches in, makes a peculiar face, and pulls out Smokey, the pet guinea pig from the second floor.

"My mistake," he says, "wrong spell." The audience claps. A tiny fairy light flickers in my mother's forget-me-not-blue eyes.

"This next illusion is extremely difficult," Marv tells us. "So I'll ask you all to be very, very quiet so I can give it my full attention."

He catches my eye and points to his watch, and I slip out of my chair.

"Don't leave me!" my mother yells after me, craning forward to try to see behind the stage curtain. "Please come back!" She's waving her arms in the air.

As if she's conjured him up, Berry, the building caretaker, emerges from behind the curtain pushing an old clothes closet on wheels. Berry has cut an extra door in it, and the crafts class has painted a big shining sun on one side and a pale quarter moon on the other.

"How many of you have ever wanted to disappear?" Marv asks. "I know I have." He makes a circle in the air with his wand and Berry rotates the closet so all four sides can be seen.

"Can you all see," asks Marv, opening the closet's front and back doors and wheeling through it, "that Mr. Marvel's cabinet is empty?"

"Yes!"

"Before I do my vanishing act," he says, "I'm going to make a beautiful girl appear, 'cause I need some good lovin'."

There's a wolf whistle from the back row. Marv shuts the front door of the cabinet and waves his magic wand: "Voilà!"

The closet wobbles from side to side, then the door bursts open and I step out—"Ta dum!"—wearing a glittery red dress and white go-go boots. Everyone claps except my mother, who is bent over her lap, folding and re-folding a paper napkin. She looks up but doesn't recognize me.

"Well, we've come to the end of our road," announces Marv, putting his arm around my waist. I can feel his whole body shaking. "Min, you come up here too, sweet thing."

My mother looks up at Marv and, for the first time in days, smiles. Then she gets up and walks to the stage, trailing little pieces of torn napkin behind her.

"You stand by me," he tells her, and she puts her hand on his shoulder.

"Can I have a drum roll?" he asks. Berry drums his fingers, bongo-style, on the side of the cupboard as we pass through the moon door. I pull it shut behind me. It's dim inside the closet and there's not much room with the wheelchair. My mother sits on Marv's knee while I squeeze in behind him. "Please help me, Jesus," he whispers.

"Ready?" Marv asks and my mother nods her head. "One... two... three... Sim sala bim!"

For a few minutes, it's like the world has gone silent. The air is so still you can taste the dust in it. Then the closet starts to spin, faster and faster. My mother is holding on tightly to Marv. I think I hear back-up singers somewhere in the distance and the beat of hands clapping.

One by one, the closet walls fall away and we're looking at the backs of the audience's heads. They're glued to their seats, speechless, gaping at the empty stage. Marv flicks a switch and his wheelchair glides toward the doors, my mother in his lap and me hitching a ride on the back.

"Open sesame," Marv commands, and the glass doors spring open. We pick up speed rolling across the snow-dusted lawn, but my mother doesn't seem to be cold. Then we lift off into the air, flying high over the river. The waves are rising and rising, licking the wheels of the chair, and just when I think we're capsizing Marv takes our hands and we float up into the friendly sky like runaway balloons. When I look over at Marv, I notice that his wheelchair is gone and he's got a pair of silver platform boots on his feet.

"*Get up, get up, get up, get up, let's make love tonight. Wake up, wake up, wake up, wake up, 'cause you do it right,*" Marv whisper-sings to my mother.

"Where are we going, Marvin?" my mother asks.

Marv's grip grows stronger, and when I look down at the hand holding mine, his skin is as smooth as a Milky Way bar. My mother's rosy lips are parted wide and her eyes are lit up like she's seeing something holy. When I look at her, it's like looking in a mirror. There's a big lump in my throat.

"It's going to be okay," Marv answers. "We're going home."

He takes off his magician's jacket and lets it go. As it falls back to earth, empty sleeves flapping and twisting in the air currents like some crazy dancing man, it turns inside out and I catch a glimpse of the nametag sewn into the lining: *Marvin Gaye—#321.*

PAUL DUTTON

OF WHICH I NEVER WOULD have imagined myself doing, never wanted to do, wouldn't have done, except that the bus I tried to take was ahead of schedule and I had to wait for the next one, which was, naturally enough, behind schedule—not that I would have been trying to catch a bus at all, except that I lost or misplaced my bicycle tire levers, a fact that came to light only after I'd expended more than the usual considerable amount of time it takes me to remove the rear wheel of my bike, wrestling with chain housing and brackets, with gear chain and wheel chain and nuts, during which efforts, as I exerted a particularly forceful pull on a recalcitrant axel-nut, the wrench slipped, causing my grip to give and my hand to fly off waywardly, violently, my forefinger meeting the sharp edge at the rusted end of the metal fender, blood from the cut mixing with the grease and grime that had accumulated on the finger in the course of the whole unlucky enterprise, which had begun when I'd come to the bike to mount and ride off on it to an appointment with a prospective client, only to find the rear tire flat, deciding impulsively then that there was time yet available to me to fix it and make my appointment, as long as I skipped the errand at the bank that I'd initially planned to complete before the appointment, having timed my departure to allow for that, which now meant that I could sacrifice the extra time in order to repair the flat, which procedure then led to my having to hasten inside and upstairs to the bathroom to wash my hands, clean and sterilize the cut on my finger, dress it with a bandage, get a latex surgical glove for the wounded hand, as protection against possible infection from the assured encounter with fresh filth and grease once I returned to the task of repairing the flat, a return delayed because the box of surgical gloves was not in its customary place in the cupboard under the bathroom sink, nor in the next likely place (the towel and linen closet), nor the next (the bedside table), nor any in a descending hierarchy of likely places, nor in an *a*scending hierarchy of *un*likely places, including hall closets, kitchen cupboards, shelves and drawers in the dining room, more shelves and drawers in the living room, boxes in the basement, the surface of and shelves above the workbench, counters and boxes in the storage room—time all the while slipping like sand between my fingers, sand that, were it so doing, would have been getting slightly bloodied by the oozing red liquid from the apparently inadequately bandaged cut, to improve which bandage I ascend again to the bathroom, where, while effecting the improvement, I chance to glance down behind the dirty-clothes hamper, noticing there the box of surgical gloves where it had somehow fallen, then snatch it up and pluck one out to wear as I return triumphantly to the shed outdoors and the completion of the flat repair, with time enough left to get it done and arrive just acceptably late at my appointment.

My appointment. He clears his throat. She sniffs. They both look pointedly at the clock. Or one of them does. Or perhaps it was me, slipping a nervous sidelong glance to see just how irritated with me they had a right to be, an irritation signalled in small ways: a gratuitous clearing of the throat, a superfluous sniff with too little energy behind it to effect the reversal of a trickle of phlegm—more a nasally inhaled sigh than a mucusy snif-fle. Or perhaps he in fact had some tiny thing caught in his throat—a particle of food from his lunch or from a mid-afternoon snack—or maybe experienced a little muscular catch, a sudden excessive flow of saliva, any number of possible other things; and maybe her sudden sharp little intake of breath was a mere respiratory spasm, or perhaps a stifled yawn, an involuntary extra little exer-tion on the drawing in of air. Probably neither of them cared or even noticed that I was—what? forty minutes late? thirty? forty-five? an hour? Anyway, if they were so busy, then however many minutes I had caused our appointment to be delayed could be viewed as extra time I had afforded them, a welcome temporal bonus to be put to good use in the pursuit of a wealth of worthwhile tasks that were theirs to complete. Shit, I was doing them a favour for chrissake, and there they were acting like I was some kind of felon or worse. Hell, I didn't cause the one bus to come early and the other late. If I could have found the damn tire levers I wouldn't even have needed to take fucking public transit. But when I got back to the shed and finally got the rear wheel off and set it against the wall, preparatory to lifting back the tire and tugging out the tube to find and patch the puncture, the tire levers turned out to have followed the surgical gloves' example in not being where they should have been, and a search of the shed turned up nothing, as did a search of the basement workroom, and searches of every other possible and impossible room they could have wandered to in the whole damn house, the seconds ticking past with each fresh area scoured, every second a unit of energy lost to futile hope, hope that drove me to throw good money after bad, temporally—metaphorically—speaking, even racing up the street and around the corner to the bike shop to buy a new set of levers, only to be greeted there by a sign in the door saying "Back in 10 minutes." That's when I decided to take the bus.

Truth be told, I don't think I would have got the damn assignment anyway. I don't think I'd even have wanted it if I'd been offered it. I can just see how it would have gone. "Oh, that's great! We just *love* your ideas. We can't *wait* to see the results." Then later, "Yes, well, but... hmmm... it's, um, it's not, uh, not really quite what we remember agreeing to." And, "Mm-hmmm, yes, I see... Yes, we realize that, but..." So, okay, I agree to re-do the whole thing according to the way they say it was supposed to be, and it's, "Better, for sure, but just here, where you..." And, "Yeah, good. Except, how about...?" Then, "Look, why not...?" And later on, "Sure, sure. You did... That's right. Yes, we did. But you haven't really..." Until finally, I'm just a tool for the execution of their own stupid ideas. And I'm supposed to have *my* name put in with a creative credit? Damned if I will. I'll make up a pseudonym and say that's what I always use for these kinds of commercial assignments... junk beneath my talents, nothing but a money-earning both-er, bloody boring, brain-dulling, soul-sapping, tedious, eyelids drooping, mind weary, body heavy, slack and swaying in the bus-seat, hand slowly slipping from where I'd rested it on my portfolio case on the seat beside me, head lolling, the hum of the motor and the voices of a nearby couple receding to the fringes of consciousness, thoughts blurring into vaguely realized associations—a recent conversation with a friend about my music, or about his; the image of my composition prof floating up out of memory's depths, expounding on form or nota-tion or formal notation or notational form; something having to do with my father; a fragment of a pop song; nothing...

I came to... slowly sluggishly, reluctantly, eyes still closed, the lush drug of a doze thick in my veins. The conversational couple was no longer on the bus. Nor, I think, were any of the other passengers who'd been there when I boarded. However long I'd been asleep, I'd wound up well past my stop. I would have to disembark now, and pay another fare to board a bus travelling in the opposite direction, back to where I should have gotten off. That, or try to talk its driver into letting me on with the wrong-way transfer I'd show him to back up my sob story.

As it chanced, I had slept my way back into that part of the city where I'd spent my childhood, an area I'd not entered since, only passing by on the main streets, in a bus or car, or on a bike. Now, in the gathering dusk, a pleasant autumn chill in the air, salmon clouds streaked with mauve bruises billowing softly against the darkening blue sky, I took in the familiar intersection, the buildings much the same, but the businesses in them utterly different: a fast-food outlet where a record store had been, a dry cleaner's displaced by a hair salon, a pet shop now a walk-in law office, a bike shop become a derelict building, and other such effects of the usual shifting commercial topography of any urban area.

I'm not given to bouts of nostalgia, but as I stood there preparing to cross to the far corner where the bus

I wanted would stop, I was taken by an uncharacteristic whim, and reversing my course, set off on a little tour through the old neighbourhood, down the hill a ways and over a few streets. The residential enclave that in those early years had pretty much circumscribed my world was, from my full-grown physical perspective, shrunk now to almost Lilliputian proportions, my neurons still bearing ghost prints from that diminutive perceptual system through which I first encountered the vast expanse of sidewalk stretching an entire city block that I covered now in a quarter of the number of strides and of minutes it had taken me then. Around a corner and a few paces away, nestled in a lot that might accommodate two average-sized houses, was a park shrunk by the passage of years to a fraction of the space it had occupied in my toddler frame of reference, when I had slid and slipped on the ice rink there in my double-bladed starter skates, after which, woollen mittens nubbed with frozen snow, feet aching with the bitterest cold, I sat wrapped up, shivering, atop a sled pulled by my big sister through the dark, along the snow-encrusted sidewalk, patiently waiting out the eternity it took her to get us to the light and warmth of home, a distance covered now in perhaps five minutes. The giant house of my childhood is a modest little structure, as I stand outside it in one spot that is two: the one this present place, the other the one where, at age ten, upon returning home from late schoolyard play, in the early autumn evening, I stopped, as my thrilled heart stopped, overcome with dreamworld excitement at seeing, through the lit living-room window, the shining dark wood of a piano newly set against the far wall, waiting for my eager fingers that could not yet span an octave, and that had so far been restricted to limited practice sessions on one of the school pianos. I'd remembered that momentous occasion—the physical fact of it—frequently over the years, but this time it came back more immediately, comprehensively—not just the sensory aspects of it, but the emotional, spiritual dimensions, which had first arrived with an intensity that perhaps had been more than I could handle at ten (as my fingers could not span an octave), and so had been closeted away until I could withstand and absorb the impact of it these decades later. I believe now—not then, not either then: not the then at ten or the then later, but now, still later, reflecting—that what I experienced as a child in that first instant of a new life with a piano in it, was the inchoate but galvanic real-ization of a calling: not just a profession, though there is that to it, but a deeper, more pressing, irreversible, even mystical, and in any case utterly indelible, imprint on the soul. At ten years of age I flew from the spot to burst into the house and (although I could not have articulated it) honour that imprint and pursue that calling. At forty or so, I strolled away from the spot, surprised, stirred, con-templative, to ramble on through the streets I'd left so long ago, and barely given a thought to since.

The circuitous route I took to the main street and its bus line led me past the grounds of my old grade school, whose grassy terraces had served as gathering place or battlefield, as our childish wishes dictated. Not only were the terraces now less imposing in height—more a gradual rise than a steep slope—but they were no longer grassy, time having shrunk finances as it had shrunk everything else in this erstwhile universe of mine, so that instead of the expanse of cropped green that carpeted the hill residing in my memory, there descended from the periphery of the schoolyard a slightly graded scattering of trees and a tangle of undergrowth.

Night had fully fallen by now, and I passed under streetlights, wrapped in memories long unvisited, surrounded by faces and names I'd thought I'd forgotten, passing here and there a house whose interior I once knew intimately, wondering about former friends who lived in them then and present strangers who lived in them now, all

BRIAN DEDORA

DURING THE PLAGUE YEARS, many of the boys died intestate, while others, with wills, had their wishes overruled in the courts by parents and siblings angered by these embarrassing deaths this punishment from god this negation of lifestyle this underbelly of sex. The property of those boys who passed without wills was entrusted to the Public Trustee, who, courted by the city's most entrepreneurial antique dealers who, with suckings and blowings of hand-warmed cash, filled their shops and galleries with the exquisite collections of these gays, who with their educated tastes had built fortifications of refinement against both the hordes at the gates howling their homophobic outrage as directed by their latest phone conversation with god and those who turned their faces away, indifferent and apathetic. Whole rooms of carved and gilded fauteuil, commodes of tulipwood marquetry and bureaux plats with ormolu and fitted embossed leather going, going, gone. Watercolours and oils in gilded encadrements stacked salon style on the walls. Portfolios of drawings and prints stashed under beds and in the backs of closets rolls of Fortuny and silks waiting for the upholsterer. In smaller rooms and modest apartments at least one or two small items of value could be acquired; a drawing, perhaps, or a curl-handled baby spoon in silver, a piece of cloisonné not large but quite fine all finding their way to the walls and glass cases of an uptown dealer.

§

I needed the room and I needed to withdraw. I could take the schmoozing for maybe a couple of hours nodding diligently and oh so knowingly at yet another somebody's being the hero of their own story. That *is* good, you've done well, and how could you, that's so clever, and you paid how much, and with whom...? I needed to withdraw. I started unloading the room by taking out the bed and the gilded headboard along with the plum-pudding mahogany chest of drawers leaving only the chandelier and a soft-padded dining-room chair inherited from some west-end apartment move and, of course, the oil painting hung dead centre on the wall opposite the window so when in daylight all I had to do was slide back the drapes to view it or, at night flick on the chandelier with the chair underneath facing the boy.

I first saw him in an uptown gallery, leaning against the wall with his back to me, and was immediately curious, so I walked over to take a closer look. I gripped the top of the stretcher and pulled him toward me and looked down over the painting and there under the dirt and the grime of so much neglect he sat surrounded by birds. I dreamt of him for three nights running. He was not for sale and I waited months to hear while the dealer negotiated his release from an estate entanglement. On obtaining a watercolour by an artist whom the dealer admired, obtained for absolutely nothing from a picker I knew, I presented it to the dealer as a small token of appreciation for his diligent work in trying to obtain the oil I dreamt about. I received the call two days later. With some under-the-table cash from a busy Christmas rush I negotiated with a gilder and framer for a carved gold frame, and a conservator for a thorough cleaning and stabilizing of the painting. The conservator suggested he'd been painted anytime from 1740 to 1760, with a possibility he might be Italian. In ten months I brought him home to my withdrawing room, cleaned, framed, and ready to hang on my specially painted silver-blonde wall.

§

He is seated, mostly naked but for the green wrap that
billows behind him and follows around to flow and con-
ceal his genitals, face on with his left foot resting on his
right knee, the right leg extended to within an inch of
the bottom of the painting. His left upper arm is held
close to his body, while the forearm is raised with palm
open fingers splayed, while his right arm is extended just
above horizontal palm down fingers again splayed; a
chameleon stands on the back of his hand. What he is sitting on is lost in the darker shadows of the painting.
What he does sit on is also obscured by two putti heads
that peer out from those shadows, one looking up to the
youth, the other, on his left, looking down and away. But
for the chameleon he is surrounded by both domestic
and exotic birds. As I view the painting. a white orange-
billed duck darts its head into the picture from the lower
right, quacking at a cluster of small parrots and budgeri-
gars while a rooster with red coxcomb and wattles pecks
at the ground with a hen beside him. Other birds whose
names I don't know stand alert with their white feath-
ered breasts plumped out, their beady eyes piercing the
gloom below and to one side of where the youth's legs
rest. Directly over his one foot, resting on the ground, a
red breasted robin and a grouse stand peering, one to the
left, the other, the grouse, to the right. A parrot in green,
orange, and white stares straight out with orange-
rimmed eyes at the viewer, standing by itself to the left
of the right foot while other birds of unknown lineage,

to me, stand perched and staring as if to pose or pounce looking left and right. They are arranged such that the patterns of their plumage contrast with the dark ground, leading to a standing barn owl with its distinctive heart-shaped face at a slight oblique to the viewer, while behind and above the owl stands the most exotic bird of all bridging the horizon and the bird-filled sky behind and above the youth. This bird is tall with dark stork-like legs and a deep umber-black plumage and white-tipped wing feathers. There is, behind his eye a red, a bright red appendage, above which and standing upright and arced from his head a gold crest. Behind him a red-headed woodpecker wings up into the air to the right as a dark blue bird with white markings flies to the left. There is a putto here in the clouds in the position of the west wind and he is blowing, as seen by the streaks of wind emanating from his mouth, while just above him an orange-beaked and black-tufted bird with dark oval eyes seemingly accuses the viewer with almost a snarl. Flying in from the left and above the chameleon is a mallard with its hen. Another, to me, unknown bird flies upward to the top of the picture ahead of them, where a bank of clouds opens to reveal another putto in the position of the north wind blowing into the parted clouds, where a duo of birds, another robin and perhaps a sparrow, emerge from the cloud, while others wing about above the youth and another, only its tail and wing tip visible, flies down out of the picture to the right. The clouds part just above and behind the youth's blonde curls. Did I mention he was blonde? His face, rounded and a bit plumpish with white rosy cheeks, hosts an aquiline nose above a closed pink mouth the same pink as his exposed nipples, and his eyes, just a bit sleepy, are turned to watch the chameleon. He is not overly handsome in a city way, but rather has the feel of a country boy, a youth from the village where the painter lived, perhaps. There is a line across the painting that cuts through his chest and his left nipple where two pieces of canvas were sewn together to get this height of canvas, about five feet by three.

§

Thinking the red ground on which the painting is painted indicated an Italian painting, I phoned reputable secondhand book dealers to conduct book searches for *Hall's Dictionary of Subjects & Symbols in Art* and his *A History of Ideas and Images in Italian Art*. The books were found but they revealed nothing about the painting, neither in image or symbol. Suggestions by others about a depiction of a saint or Francis of Assisi were all but ridiculous, as saints are not depicted mostly naked with a wrap sliding over where everybody looks. Nothing about the birds either in any specific way, although there was a reference to the chameleon and the Gonzagas of Northern Italy, which scent caused my heart to quicken but went slowly downbeat to nowhere. A chance

encounter with one of those friend-of-a-friend situa-
tions at a small dinner party and an invitation to describe
the painting led to one of the guests practically jumping
from his table place saying, "No, no, not Italian, Spanish,
it came from La Corunna, I was there when the crate
was opened!" "Back up, back up, start from the beginning, and tell me." My heart beating with the quick of
the hunt resumed.

§

"Manolo and his lover came here in the seventies. He
was a designer. You know, doing apartments, gathering
harlequin sets and getting them re-upholstered, matching
this and matching that. Did design for some furniture
companies. Absolutely wild in that Spanish way, a bit
over the top for this place but everybody loved him, you
know. His lover was such a nice guy but hey it was the
seventies, right, bad clothes, bad music, but lots of clubs.
Anyway, he was doing well and they went back home on
vacation and must have got the painting because it
arrived about two months later. I was there at the ware-
house when they opened it up; it was fabulous, so rich
and European-looking and nothing like the stuff around
here. There it was out of its wrap, we taking turns with a
camera posing beside it until off they went in somebody's van. He was one of the first in the city to go.
Christ, if we'd only known. Then his lover came down

with it. Yimmy, that's it! His name was Jimenez but he couldn't say the *j* it was a *y* so we nicknamed him. Who knows what happened with all their things, the place was packed to the rafters. The painting hung in the dining room opposite this polished sideboard, everybody wanted to sit facing it, and as the wine bottles piled up the theories about its meaning piled up too. We were too pissed, I'd like to come and see it... maybe I could find the photos." "Yeah."

§

The insight, if you could call it that, occurred in the cab on the way home from the airport. I'd just flown in from the interior on a night flight after my father's funeral eleven months after my mother's. She'd had a couple of small strokes before the big one finally claimed her. I phoned one night and she asked, "Whoever thought it would end like this...?" My brother found our father on the kitchen floor, fallen victim to a massive brain hemorrhage. I don't drive; I don't even own a car and don't want to. I take cabs, enjoying, especially at night, sitting in the dark back seat with my cellphone turned off, the preliminaries with the driver over, watching neighbourhoods and people drift by. Their mimed animations beyond the rain-dribbled windows: a dope-deal in the throat of an alley, some rain-soaked kids running, a grim dark huddle at a bus stop. Withdrawing from the horizontal, I become vertical, and steal a chance to sit with myself and my thoughts; solitude being so hard to achieve, I take it where I can, and in the silence arrive where the hard irritant at the core of this resides. I was thinking about being an orphan in the world and what would eventually be my own death, when the painting in absolute clarity came into my mind, and with it its sad readily apparent metaphor, which if it didn't hurt so much, would be, almost, pathetic. He is all of us in our optimistic youth, sitting earthbound, while all around him the birds of the air, birds of the North and West wind elude him with their exotic free flight, or their pedestrian domestic pecking, as he gazes at the chameleon that can change, at will, its colours. I cannot change my colours, and I cannot fly but in my dreams, sweet dreams the closest from time.

BRIAN EVENSON

IT WAS AN OLD HOUSE, the sort of place she could afford since the divorce. A simple Denver square, a main level and then a converted attic, its walls upstairs paper-thin and uninsulated. She took the downstairs bedroom, giving her son the run of the upstairs: two rooms with sloping ceilings, a bathroom, a built-in closet.

Except for her couch and the beds which a former college roommate helped her with, she didn't have any help moving in. Otherwise, she wrestled things out of her old place and into a rented van and then out of the truck again and into the new place. After three days of this, she was exhausted, but also finished.

She fetched her boy from school in the van, filthy still in her moving clothes.

"Is it done?" he wanted to know. "Can I see it now? Are we sleeping there tonight?"

Yes, she said, it was finished, they would sleep there tonight. There were still boxes everywhere but that didn't matter, they would clean things and put them away and then it would be home.

When they got back she showed him the upstairs, then left him to unpack and explore. Then she went downstairs to lie down, to gather a moment's rest before opening the next box.

§

She was first aware something had gone wrong when, still half-asleep on the couch, she heard a strange thumping as her son came down the stairs. She sat up and gathered herself and waited for him to arrive, but he stopped at the bottom of the stairs and waited, stood there just out of sight.

"Mommy?" he finally said, his voice slightly quavery.

"Honey," she said, "what is it?" When, after a moment, he still didn't respond, she stood and crossed to the doorway.

He was sitting on the bottom tread, face pale, dazed. He looked normal, no blood anywhere, no bruises. But one of his arms was strange—normal down to the elbow, but from the elbow down no longer a child's arm but incredibly swollen, enlarged, an adult arm.

He was staring at it, kept opening and closing the fingers.

"Oh, God," she said, and he began to look as if he might cry.

"It's not my fault," he said. "I didn't do it."

"Didn't do what?" she asked. Very slowly, she sat down beside him and took his forearm in her hand, began to examine it. "Was there a bee?" she asked. "Did something bite you?"

"No," he said, and indeed she couldn't see any sign of a sting or a bite. The forearm, she saw now, holding it, wasn't swollen at all, was instead just what it had first seemed to be, the forearm not of a six-year-old but of a male in his late teens, muscled, skin lightly dusted with hair.

"What did you do?" she asked again.

"It wasn't my fault," he said again.

She looked at the arm more closely. Yes, nothing unhealthy about it; it just looked like part of a normal adult arm that had, somehow, been grafted onto her boy in place of his own.

"I don't understand," she said.

He began to cry and she picked him up and held him, his strange arm hanging limply. She rocked him and rubbed his back until he calmed down.

"Does it hurt?" she asked later.

He shook his head.

"That's good anyway," she said. "Now, can you tell me about it?"

"I just reached in the closet," he said. "All I did was reach in the closet."

§

She found him a juice box and then seated him on the couch. She found the TV and carried it in and stacked it on some boxes and plugged it in. He sat holding the juice box in his adult hand, having to concentrate to get the arm to bring it to his mouth.

She called his pediatrician on her cellphone, whispered to the nurse what had happened, waited on the telephone until the doctor finally came.

"And does he have a temperature?" he asked.

"No," she said, "no temperature."

"And it doesn't hurt?"

"He says it doesn't hurt," she said. "It doesn't seem to."

"It's swollen?"

"Not swollen exactly. Just bigger."

"He has allergies?"

"I don't think so."

There was a brief silence. "I'd like to see it," he finally said, and there was a strange wonder in his voice. "I don't have the slightest notion of what it could be. Tell you what. I'm on call at the hospital tonight; why don't you bring him there in a few hours and page me? If it gets worse, just bring him sooner."

She checked him. He was still watching the staticky TV, holding the juice box. The arm didn't look quite as big now, or perhaps that was wishful thinking.

Upstairs, the rooms were exactly as she had remembered them, simple rooms, ordinary, with sloping walls. The closet door, she saw, could be locked from the outside. She opened it. It seemed just an ordinary closet, a floor of large slats of unfinished wood, walls of pasteboard covered in some sort of whitewash. It smelled musty, but that was hardly extraordinary: it was an old house.

Carefully, she stuck one hand in. Nothing extraordinary, she thought, nothing happening.

But then suddenly the hand began to tingle and she saw her knuckles begin to thicken, the fingers becoming more bony, the skin becoming more delicate, liver-spotted. She jerked her hand out and looked at it. It was no longer her hand, but the hand of an old woman.

§

Her boy was still watching TV. Dazed, she sat down beside him, cradling her hand as if it were a baby or a small animal. *What's wrong with me?* she wondered. *Why am I not screaming?*

"You're not to go into the closet again," she said. "Promise me."

"It wasn't my fault," he said, and looked a little afraid.

"It wasn't your fault," she assented. "But don't go in again. We'll nail it closed once I unpack the hammer."

He nodded, went back to watching TV. She turned, watched with him. *What's wrong with me?* she thought. *Should I go to a doctor too?* she wondered. *How am I going to explain this?*

§

After another hour or so, still stunned, still sitting in front of the TV, she was sure of it: his arm was shrinking, slowly going back to normal. It was no longer an adult arm now, nor yet a pudgy child's arm, but in some mid-pubescent state between. Her hand too felt a little better, looked a little better as well, the liver spots slowly fading. It was probably, she told herself, going to be okay.

§

When the doorbell rang, it surprised her. The boy's arm was still not back to normal but was closer now, just a little off, as if puffy or swollen. She got up and went to open the door.

Her ex-husband was on the porch.

"Oh," she said, "what are you doing here?"

"I've been waiting outside for him for fifteen minutes. That's the arrangement," he said. "I shouldn't have to see you. I shouldn't have to be talking to you like this."

"Sorry," she said, "I'm busy moving. I forgot you were coming."

"I'm coming as a favour to you, remember?" he said, shaking his head.

"Sorry," she said. "It's just, this day—"

"Is he ready?"

"Nearly," she said. "I'll get him ready quickly. Do you want to come in?"

"No," he said, lips tight. "I don't want to come in. But I don't particularly want to wait out here either. So I'll come in."

She opened the door a little wider and turned away, went back to the living room. "Honey," she said. "Your father's here."

The boy looked away from the TV and waved, then went back to watching.

"What's wrong with his arm?" said the husband. "It's swollen."

"What?" she said. "Nothing, just a little accident. It's going back to normal."

But he was already at the couch, grilling the boy. *It wasn't my fault*, the boy kept saying, *it wasn't my fault*.

"But it has to be somebody's fault," her ex-husband was saying. "Doesn't it? Was it Mommy's fault?"

"Hey," she said, "what do you think—"

"What did Mommy do to you?" he said, his voice rising.

She was speaking faster now, on the defensive, trying to explain: it was the closet. The closet, he was shouting, how could it be the closet? Had he caught his arm in it? Wasn't that impossible? Wasn't that the same lie as 'he fell down the stairs'? What was he accusing her of, she wanted to know. Could he really believe that she had done this? *Irresponsible,* he muttered, *you've always*—But she herself just couldn't believe that he could ever think that she would hurt a hair on this child's—

But no, he wasn't listening. He had already decided what had happened, that she was at fault: it fit with the paranoid sense of the world he had developed and with his resentment for her having left him. It was why she had divorced him. Her son just kept looking back and forth between the two of them, silent. She was yelling, she realized, and her ex-husband was yelling back, and at some point he took out his cellphone and started taking pictures of the boy's arm, making him hold the other arm next to it for contrast.

And then he had gathered up the boy and had hustled him out to the car and she stood at the doorway exhausted and frustrated, watching them go.

But once the boy was in the car her ex-husband came angrily striding back.

"I don't know what's going on exactly," he said, "but I know it's not good."

"Nothing's going on," she said.

"There's clearly abuse here," he said. "Just look at his arm. You need help."

"This is so crazy," she said. "This is just about trying to hurt me."

His lips tightened. "All I know is that something's happened to the boy and that it happened under your care. That makes you responsible. How can you expect me to release him into your care until I'm certain it won't happen again?"

"Release him into my care?" she said. "What's that supposed to mean?"

"It means I'm not bringing him back until I know he'll be safe. I have photos, I have proof. This time I'm the one in charge." And with that he turned on his heel and left.

§

She went back into the house and washed her face and tried to calm down. It was crazy, she told herself, he had gone crazy, and once he'd had a few hours to think it out he'd realize how wrong he'd been and bring the child back. The child belonged with her, the court had said as much. This just proved they'd been right. Besides, in a few hours the arm would be back to normal and the boy would tell his father the truth and everything would be okay.

By the next morning her own hand had returned to normal. But he still had the boy. She called his cell and left a message, suggesting it had all been a misunderstanding and perhaps they could work it out. If he could just let her explain. He didn't call back. She called a few more times, kept getting voicemail. She waited, calling later from a pay phone so he wouldn't know it was her. He picked up and then hung up as soon as he heard her voice.

What was there for her to do, what were her options? She could call the police, accuse him of kidnapping. That would get her the child back, but would make their future interactions even more complicated. She could try to reason with him, but how could she reason with him if she couldn't talk to him? She could wait for him to come to his senses, but how long would that take?

And then she had an idea. She pressed it down at first, but it kept coming back to her, until she was finally thinking, why not? It would solve everything for good. Why not?

§

She drove to the boy's school, pulled him out of class in the middle of the day, and drove him home.

"Why can't I stay?" he wanted to know. His arm, she saw, was normal now, the same arm as always.

"I need you at home, sweetheart," she said. "I'm sorry."

He just ducked his head, went back to fiddling with his book bag.

At home she got him some lunch, set him up in front of the TV. She stationed herself against the wall where she could see out the front window, could also keep her eye on the clock.

When it was time for him to be getting out of school, she turned off the TV. He complained a little.

"But it's such a nice day," she said. "You should go play."

"But I don't want to go play," he said.

"The people who sold me the house said there were gophers in the back yard," she lied.

"Gophers," he said.

"Yes," she said. "They said if you walk around after a while they start popping up. There are also some squirrels living in the garage."

"Really?" he said.

"Really," she said. "But you have to be patient. You have to go outside and be patient."

§

Not long after she coaxed her son outside, her husband arrived, bursting in, looking crazed.

"Where is he?" he asked.

"I have him," she said. "He stays here."

"You can't have him," he said, taking her by the arm and shaking her. "You aren't safe. Where is he?"

She waited for what she thought would be the right amount of time and then turned her face away.

"Are you sure it has to be this way?" she asked.

His grip loosened a little.

"I'm sure," he said.

"Can't we go talk to someone about it?" she asked. "Go together and speak with someone?"

"Absolutely not," he said. And then added, "It's for his own good."

"He's upstairs," she claimed.

He looked at her once and let go of her, then started up the stairs, calling the boy's name. She followed.

He went from the first room to the second room to the bathroom before turning back on her, his face contorting.

"Where is he?" he asked.

"He was up here," she said. "He's still here somewhere. Maybe he's in the closet."

§

But of course when he opened the closet the boy wasn't there. Her ex-husband saw just what she had seen: an ordinary closet with an unfinished pine floor, walls of whitewashed pasteboard, empty.

Or at least empty when he first opened it. For as soon as he opened it, she shoved him as hard as she could and he stumbled in.

She tried to get the door closed on him and mostly did, except for his hand. She held the door shut against the hand with all her might as he tried to get back out. At first he shouted angrily, telling her not to be a child and then, suddenly, a strange fear came into his voice and he was screaming now, first *Let me out, let me out*, and then words that were no longer coherent and no longer really words. He pushed against the door with less and less force, then his hand spasmed beside her face. His voice grew hoarser and more and more wavery and then stopped altogether.

Very carefully she released enough pressure from the door to be able to push his hand, fingers curling now, in. Then she closed the door the rest of the way and waited. When she opened the door again, just to look in, the closet was empty; a little dustier perhaps, but empty. She closed the door, and locked it.

§

She went downstairs and into the bathroom, straightening herself in the mirror. Brushing back her hair, she stared at her face. Did she look any different? How had she changed? But no, she looked the same as she always did, she thought, which somehow frightened her.

She heard a door open and shut. The house was new enough that she felt her heart flutter a moment before she heard her son's voice and realized it had not been the closet door she'd heard at all. He came in and stood in the doorway of the bathroom.

"What is it, Honey?" she asked.

"I can't find any gophers," he said.

"That's too bad, Dear," she said. "Maybe you'll have better luck tomorrow."

He sighed and wandered out into the living room. She stayed where she was, still looking at the mirror.

"Is that Dad's car?" he asked.

"Is it?" she said absently.

"Is he here?"

"He's not in here," she said. "Maybe he just got here. Why don't you go out and see?"

She heard the front door open as he went out, and only then did she dare let go of the sink and make her way to the living room, arranging herself carefully on the couch as he opened the door and came back in.

"He's not there," he said.

"Not there?" she said. "How strange," and gave her best smile.

"Where's Daddy?" he said. And when she didn't answer, said it again. *Where's Daddy?*

"Oh, Honey," she said, "Sweetie. Daddy had to go away."

He kept asking questions and she kept answering them absently, waiting for them to stop so that she could think. She would nail the door shut, she was thinking. She'd have the closet covered over. *Everything would be better now,* she told herself as she held her now howling son and stroked his back. *Everything would be just fine.*

JOHN RIDDELL

"Could anything be more insane
than for the human race to die out
because we 'couldn't afford' to save ourselves?"
— John Hotson, Professor Emeritus of Economics

THE CLOCK READS 12:45—but is it a.m. or p.m.?

I lie on my bed eyes focused on the motionless ceiling fan.

The rooming house corners a major downtown intersection. The ebb and flow of traffic is controlled by traffic lights. I can watch the interplay from my bedroom window, a small window so loose-fitting that a wedge of wood must be placed between frame and sill if it is to remain open. A fire escape extends from the third floor (overhead) down past the window (in question) to the ground (below).

Directly across the room from the window, the left frame of a door is set in some four feet from the east wall. The left edge of a (medium sized) table stands six inches to the right of the right frame of this door.

Numerous sheets of paper are scattered over a tabletop. (A few have dropped to the floor.) It is a book I'm working on, 'Towards a General Theory of Economics.' Did you know that after hundreds of years, we still do not have a *workable* economic theory?

There is another table adjacent to this one, covered with a soiled red/white checkered tablecloth. A toaster sits on the table, a bit to the left of a computer monitor. A half-empty jar of marmalaide stands midway between the monitor and a keyboard; and towards the side of the table opposite the wall, a knife and fork rest on a dirty plate (exhibiting: a dash of ketchup, a bit of jam, several chicken bones, etc.).

These days are frightening. There is no social or environmental accountability. Speaking of economics, national governments have shifted allegiance to the for-profit (market) sector, away from the public (not-for-profit) sector, that is, the very citizens who elected them. It is a part of my thesis: a symptom of the disease of *economic determinism*: a myopia which kills. (It will be further detailed in Chapter 3 of the book.)

Should access to the hallway be required, the dead-bolt lock on the door must be released, but never immediately. The hallway may be empty but this is not always the case: at this very moment (or at some other) someone may be passing by and/or talking to someone else. A moment or two taken, then, to listen by the door *may* determine if there is any audible activity in the hallway. Even if no such activity is detected, it is still possible that a conversation is in fact underway in *whispered* tones, tones too low to hear from within a bedsitting room; or it may be that someone is lingering, listening in silence, for whatever the reason may be. (Some tenants do not get along all that well with others; indeed, some believe there is a sinister element at play on the premises...)

It is early on in the afternoon.
It is almost time to go.

A closet, adjacent to the window, stores old boxes, books, momentos of the past, (perhaps future dreams), piled up on the floor in a mish-mash of organized neglect. A pair of brown trousers lies folded on the upper shelf. The trousers are so well worn I think I may dispose of them. Below the shelf, on a clothes rack which extends the four-foot width of the closet, an assortment of shirts and jackets hang, including a plaid shirt. (The black and blue woollen jacket hanging next to it is fairly new, but would be too warm for this time of year.) The plaid shirt is lifted from the clothes rack. The hallway may indeed be empty now, but it is too risky to chance.

The fire escape has worked loose from the side of the building, so it is necessary to grip the railing securely while descending, as the structure wobbles slightly. The walkway at the side runs west to a main thoroughfare, and east through a small rectangular back yard, containing a modest vegetable garden along its north boundary, and a woodshed at the rear, just to the left of the landlord's garage.

My thesis is two-fold: (i) that 'mainstream' economics serves as little more than a *decoy*, designed to legitimate the excessive lifestyles of some three percent of the world's population, at the expense of the rest of us, other species, and the environment; (ii) that our economy is composed of <u>three primary sub-systems</u>: the for-profit (market) sector; the not-for-profit (public) sector; and the environment; that each of these subsytems is *radically* different from each other in purpose and delivery; and that each must function in-relation to the others in order for the whole (economy) to function properly. None of this is discussed in so-called 'mainstream' economics. You see where I'm going?

In fact the walkway skirts the south boundary of the aforementioned back yard, and terminates at a lane which runs at right angles to it, north and south the length of the block, and extends further north for three blocks to a main thoroughfare, past a residential sector containing numerous highrise dwellings, the occasional variety store, a large church sequestered on the edge of a park, a subway intersection, a shopping plaza, and so on.

None of these were here years ago.

I know.

I've lived in this area for a long time. I moved here after my wife died.

Now I have arrived at my destination.

Recessed lights are set into a low (black) ceiling, and function in concert with several heavily shaded lamp units hung at regular intervals along (red) walls. This lighting arrangement serves to accentuate rather than alleviate the shadows in the room. (Perhaps this is the effect desired by the owners.)

The pub is 'T'-shaped. The stem of the 'T' being the main serving area (some forty feet wide), sprinkled with four-foot square brown tables each holding an ashtray, a salt shaker, and each accompanied by three straight-backed metal chairs. The bar is located in the left segment of the crossbar of the 'T', along with additional tables. Further tables, a shuffleboard, washrooms, a dart board and a small Boston table, are to be found in the right segment of the crossbar of the 'T.' And yet in spite of its considerable diversions, this pub is not particularly popular: it is frequented almost exclusively by older males, males who live alone, who have few if any friends or acquaintances other than those they see here every day.

How sad to see people live this way, in such isolation.

The problem I am currently working on has to do with the funding of the *public* sector. Tax dollars alone won't suffice. Over the last forty years the public sector has rapidly expanded, and rightly so. Nation-state central banks could be used to assist in funding public sector programs (such as health care) or infrastructure projects (such as subway extensions). This would not cause inflation, as the monies would be *absorbed* into costs incurred. For example, hospitals could be built (not torn down); doctors, nurses and technicians could be trained (not laid off). All the resources, the people-power exist: *the only missing ingredient is money*. Of course bank reserves would have to be re-instated. They were and again could be a powerful inflation inhibitor.

Slightly to the right of the junction of the stem of the 'T' with its crossbar, there is a wooden platform built out from the wall, some six above the floor. Upon it sits a tv set which can be seen and heard from anywhere in the room. A new arrival has taken his customary seat.

'Frenchie,' the waiter currently on duty, approaches him, asks him how he is.

"Fine."

"Good."

'Frenchie' (none of us know his real name) places draught beer on the table, accepts a small tip, duly thanks the customer, then moves on into the darkness in search of further sales. The new arrival sits back, savours half a glass of draught, lights a cigarette, glances at the tv overhead: at this time each weekday, the same game show is on.

The years 1945-1970 were the best twenty-five years of the twentieth century. Did you know that? Jobs were aplenty, technology appeared to be promising shorter work weeks. We were on the way. A large part of the reason for such prosperity was the intelligent use of our central bank, which helped get us out of the Great Depression, helped finance the war years, and helped to build our national infrastructure. In the 70s, things changed. Market forces reasserted themselves at the expense of our socio-environmental needs. It's been downhill ever since.

What time is it?

On a pillar above the rectangular group of tables at the back of the tavern there is a large clock, but the time it registers is obscured by the pervasive dimness and the cloud of smoke which hangs like a perpetual fog in the motionless air. (Everyone here, including staff, smoke heavily: they pay no heed to warnings from the outside world.)

Those sitting nearby (may) note that, at the moment, the clock reads 2:48, but bear in mind that its time is never precise due to the continual sixty-second sweeps the (red) second hand inscribes across the bland (white) face and (black) numerical script which constantly (*every second!*) infers the current time...

... Clock time is a necessary evil. The psychological (manmade) concept of time is an illusion: the memories of yesterday; and the expectations for tomorrow. These closets of time will close in on us, suffocate us, even kill us—if we let them.

In the nineteen-thirties, during the Great Depression, the banks were in the doghouse. That history has been repressed. Back then regulation, it was agreed, was not a 'consideration': it was a *necessity*. Deregulation and Globalization became the buzzwords of the seventies and eighties. Look what's happened. A social and planetary disaster. D&G are simply codewords for excess without accountability. (I will expand upon this, along with examples, in Chapter 8 of my book.)

On sunny days a slice of sunlight slips into the tavern through the front windows in the lunchroom, the latter being no longer in service. In fact this tavern used to be very popular, full of life and laughter. But business here has declined steadily. I doubt if they can survive much longer. Likely the property will be converted into condominiums, or some such. People nowadays live in stacked rectangular cells, effectively sealed off from each other and the outside world. There are more and more of these. They grow higher and higher, blocking out the sky. Albert Camus saw it coming: "The world will no longer be divided between just and unjust, but masters and slaves."

A waiter has placed some beer on a table at the rear of the pub. This fresh cold draught sports a frothy head about a quarter-inch deep and two-and-a-half inches in diameter. Below this froth, golden beer extends some five inches to the bottom of the (fluted) glass. The crackling foam capping the draught diminishes rapidly. The sides of the glass, by the way, are lightly frosted, and of course the frost condenses; consequently, sporadic beads of water run down the glass, merge with other beads and stream down the glass until halted by the table, whereupon a thin circle of water forms which if not wiped clean will stain the tabletop...

I often bring a bit of work along. I write: "The Meteor, which traumatized us socially, was the Industrial Revolution. It caused a catastrophic upheaval, *separating* the private sector (the market) from the public sector. In fact, the market transcended the very society which engendered it: *markets have come to control society, rather than society controlling markets*. For some two hundred years this cancerous wound has metastatized, such that what we have today might be termed *Advanced Market Supremacy*. Mainstream economics today defines environmental stewardship and public sector needs as 'externalities' with disastrous results... As to the environment, public/private patnerships need to be developed, with stringent regulations and target dates, subject to severe penalty if not adhered to." (I intend to include a Chapter on suggested protocols.)

One can observe in each draught glass a stream of hundreds (thousands?) of bubbles rising to the surface, bursting. Over time, this activity dissipates: (i) the exterior frost evaporates, dries; (ii), the interior stream of bubbles subsides. The glass soon stands without incident, a motionless gold *icon*, set against a slice of sun, cutting through shadows...

But even the sun, someday, will die.

It is 3:45 pm.

At four o'clock each weekday there is a movie on channel two.

There is change on one of the tables and four empty draught glasses. 'Frenchie' replaces the old with the new.

The four o'clock movie is a boring western.

"Boring," someone says.

"Yes," another echoes.

... It would be easy enough to turn the channel selector, find some other, more suitable program. However that is not an option; it has been the routine now for many (how many?) years...When the movie ends at six o'clock, an informal break may be in order: some patrons return to their rooms within the hotel, others to rooms nearby; some must travel farther to get to where they live; and of course there are always those who stay on, consider a break to be unecessary, at least for the time being...

The sun has or (depending on the time of year) is about to set. Were it warmer, it would be appropriate to nap for a while in a nearby park. Presently it is too cold.

People do not understand how money is created. I call it the "Best Kept Secret of the 20th Century." Most people think there is something like a big barrel of it, and that once you run out, you run out. That is not so. Chapter 7 will argue that an understanding of the money-creation function — *how* money is created, *who* creates it, and for what *purposes* — is the very foundation upon which a workable, equitable "General Theory of Economics" must be built!

... By using the fire escape to gain access to the building rather than the front door, chance meetings with tenants, visitors, or the landlord are foregone. A second floor bedsitting room window has been left propped open. Cross-corner from the window, a refrigerator set to the right of a stove stands with its back against the outer side of the back wall of the closet, its right edge flush with the edge of that wall. In the refrigerator there are some cold cuts, cheese, onions, and bread, each wrapped in plastic; a dish of butter, a bottle of ketchup (half empty), a jar of mayonnaise (half full), pickles, olives, etc.

Sandwiches can readily be made from these ingredients.

I write: "We may have irreversibly changed the chemical balance of Mother Earth. All reputable scientists now agree that, given current warming trends, the Arctic, Antarctic and Greeland ice will disappear within fifty years. So it is now possible to argue *with credibility* that the next generation, or the one after that, *may be the last*. We can only exist within a certain temperature range. The hottest ten years on record have all occurred in the last fourteen years, last year being the hottest ever..."

There is a dresser against the south wall of the bed-sitting room, several feet to the left of the window. Between it and the bed there is a lamp on a small night table. When switched on (as it is now) it casts a pool of light on the ceiling. Across the top of the lampshade is a three-pronged wire crossbar, its three extensions bounded by the rim at the top of the lampshade; all three extensions converge into a small central hub, secured by a connecting knob at the apex of the hooped wire lampshade. But the three-pronged wire crossbar is quite thin, and the bulb wattage is so high that the light emanating from the bulb overlaps the locations where the crossbar's shadow should be, in effect erasing it so completely that not a single trace of it appears on the ceiling within the context of that pool of light where it *must* appear—if it is to appear anywhere at all.

A profound misunderstanding of the interplay of market, social, and environmental sub-systems causes most poverty, illness, war, and global warming. Outer space is not 'the final frontier': it is an understanding of economics and its Earthly applications. The general population knows more about physics than it does about economics.

That is why Part III of the book offers "Solutions," such as electric car production, subsidized or financed through national central banks. Another solution involves vegetarian lifestyles, as they reduce ground, water, and crop pollution. We are not carnivores! The bowels of humans and carnivores are strikingly different. Carnivores don't get colon cancer from meat diets, as we do.

Workable solutions exist.

At the moment (there is no other time) a clock in a room somewhere reads 7:45. It could be 7:45 in the morning, or in the evening of today, yesterday, the next day, or the day after that. It could be any time at all, any day, any year, anywhere: an indifferent witness to any given event (a personal victory, perhaps, or a collective defeat). But whatever the moment may be, its Being is *instantly* erased by the relentless sweep of the second hand, which passes in continual radial arcs across the clock's motionless face, time and time again.

Did you know that most people equate who they are with what they think? It has been shown that most thought-content is illusory, fear-based and repetitive, and tends to gravitate around past (identity) and future (expectations). But these modes have no existence! Thought-structures are thus often equivalent to dream-states. It may (almost?) be argued that "I think, therefore I am *not*."

In the final section I will explore the notion of 'separation' (ego) as a social *phantasm*: I am *not* 'someone' *apart from* what *is*. In relation to that, I hope to show how *the trance of thought* has contributed significantly to our socio-economic malaise, and to the environmental crisis we have created. I will also offer what I hope will be some contribution towards workable solutions.

I look out the window at sky, trees, the sun, passing traffic. No matter what may happen a grand, mysterious Beauty is always here.

I glance at the clock. It is 8:00 a.m.

I have to go now.

I must get back to work.

STUART ROSS

IT WAS HERE THAT YOU found me. Here that you found me perched in a tree that ran from the ground. As if it were fleeing the very ground that squeezed it towards the sky, grunting and straining. But it didn't reach the sky. The tree, not the ground. It reached considerably lower and in its branches I perched until you found me. I pointed and your eyeballs rolled down my biceps, gathering speed on my forearms, onto my wrists, my hands, my index fingers.

I said, "See? Like I said."

It was a kind of light out that was dark. That kind after the oceans ended. A dark of dead fish in the day. In the day, the shopping carts, their creaking, the horrible screees they hurled into the pitch.

"My mama used to put milk in them," you said.

"Plus Snickers."

"Snickers if I was good. Plus tins of soup of several varieties."

Soup was a thing I remembered. Now the shopping carts rattled and squealed across the land made so much bigger. Through the streets, no person to push them. The sky weighed more than it ever had and rooftops collapsed beneath the weight. Shopping carts prowled in lurching packs.

Some leaves, some twigs. No soup. A feather from a bird that sailed. A feather that sailed from the clouds. The clouds swam naked through the thick sky and we heard a bell, the sound of one, like a crying.

"What's on TV?" you asked.

"What's a TV?"

"On."

"Oh, on. I remember that girl who danced a lot with the bosom. Plus police that always did funny things."

You nodded like there was electricity. We perched together in the tree where you found me, the sky draped over us like a gigantic lung. You wore a tie but I did not wear a tie. Beneath us, shopping carts. In the distance, other trees, with us in them. Us in them, one with tie, one without, there were no other options, the sky a gigantic lung.

Screee.

As far as the eye could see. From the tips of my fingers.

"I invince you," you said.

"I can't—"

"I don't let you beat me."

The sky shuddered and undulated and your palm hit my shoulder. I hate that part. Not my shoulder—your palm hitting it. I hate the palm of your hand against my shoulder—the part when that happened. The clatters and squeals of the shopping carts grew louder.

I crouched in the closet, draped in a bird sheet. A bed-sheet with birds. Not quite. More precisely, I hurtled from the branch of a tree, draped in a huge slab of sky.

You said again, from further away, "I don't let you beat me."

The thing you said. It got smaller while the shopping carts got bigger. I stayed more or less the same size, with subtle fluctuations.

It seemed unfortunate that after hanging on so long, fishless day after fishless day, the air drawing charcoal smudges beneath my eyes, I should receive your flat hand to where my arm was attached. Where my arm was attached, but up the neck a bit, I thought of a pun involving folly and falling but was unable to build a satisfying narrative around it.

I could smell the screee of the cart that, shopping, caught me. For sure I could hear it. How things had changed. From my papa's time, and the time of his papa in the shtetl, but also from just thirty seconds ago. I felt the cold metal frame of the shopping cart press at my knees and my shoulders. I clutched the cage of it. I clutched its cage and the squealing came from me now, my wheels, my rusting castors. Didn't matter. No matter.

I was a tin of soup.

I was Snickers if I was good.

I was a feather, a leaf.

You could hear them spasm and creak in every dark of the light, and that was me.

MELODY SUMNER CARNAHAN

YOU ARE SO EROTIC YOU are the most erotic person i have
ever met you are the most erotic person who has ever
lived you are like a goddess i have wanted to do this for
twenty years ever since i met you ever since i first saw
you i wanted to kiss you i wanted to touch you ever
since i first saw you since i first met you you are so erotic you are the most erotic person i know you are a goddess you are the most erotic person to me you don't
know how long i've wanted to do this i have been wanting to do this for a hundred years i've wanted to touch
your body are you offended does this offend you are you
offended by this you want me to stop you can tell me if
you want me to stop what oh don't think about that
don't worry about that this is perfect you are so erotic
you have no idea how long i've wanted to do this yes
that's good you aren't offended by this this is something

i've wanted to do for eons for millennia with you i wanted to kiss you before i got too old you want me here yes everything is fine everything is perfect this is the most erotic thing on earth it's just right it's just perfect this is my favourite thing i wanted to do this with you i knew this was my chance before i got too old i was afraid i was too old yes you want this i never do this with anyone i only want to do this with you you are so erotic it's just right oh that's fine you are so fine to do this yes it's oh so fine you are the one i want you are this is oh so nice my oh my do you like it too you do it so right you are oh so nice oh my oh my how come i waited so long.

THE MOMENT:

The rain began the moment the transport departed *after days and nights of deep crushing hugs and entwinement,* it was the first and last time one disappeared down that lane *has to say goodbye is no good at it* five in the morning dawning of weeks before *the two separated at birth* pushing down onto the bed that first night then out the door the last *promised, well, promised too but changed mind* inviting back in to briefly sleep hands interlaced bracing for the morning's separation.

Of all the sudden ones in the severed-head universe were the first most happy most mature in that instance for sure *wondered how was doing now never to return* five kinds of love six kinds of restraint, bodies puppets to the ventriloquist dummies of brains, lip-synching statistics to the sound of unrecorded personal histories wishing only to be simple, to be here: the two talking into the wind, ripples on the lake light fading, born to the same singularity, male speaking with voices of children and authority, female revealing three halves of self in perpetuity.

Skirt and tights pulled down below the knees then off completely *surprised it was that easy*, mouth on saying *is it time to go? a few more minutes, no* the zipper broken and the rules one by one. The glad ripping apart of the almost-never of that exact unexpected moment.

Had been giving each day to the demanding demons food and drink. Studying the manual for continuous existing. When the transport pulled away, war-torn, heart sore, one walked the perimeter where night before galaxies of infidels celebrated the ending of supremacy in that sector. All had seemingly exited without notice, as in a rapture. The Shy left door wide open, bathroom fan flaring noisily, lights ablaze, crushed cigarettes all over the place, urgent to restore her empire. At Picasso's half an uneaten meat pie on the floor next to gaping beers spilled party pillows empty rum and bourbon bottles hastily relocated broken furniture. The Young One's room smelled sweet like her but hardly anyone had done what they had been asked for.

Likely will meet again how say that knowing impossible floating not thinking lay down awaiting knock at door. The Glamorous returning clipboard along with Welder's roller and various malleable metals papered over with stickers as instructed, *Oh so finally did it together, eh? No, but given enough time yes,* honest in that moment, boombox roaring.

Transport gone half-an-hour rain gained intensity. Went where before there had been many gone now on depleted planet. Alone. Lonely. All will blossom and suffer, all blossom in suffering. Oh hell, why not die now everything has been so exhausted satisfying. The world as metaphor for what escapes understanding. What means? Don't know but *earlier asked if reminded of anyone said no but did remind of first in school who was also a little crazy and who had changed* the way of seeing real in the unreal moment to moment.

That final day fire-making and range-training keep eyes from exchanging clinging unreason. Welder's shop redolent of paint and glue fearless with bandsaw no goggles smoking furious wooden tombstones uncharted territory. Ryoanji at piano: I am so lusty, shaking head then, oh I mean *rusty!* Hilars shared spanking play as graceful Nymph rounding corner glances through window at two collapsing in a heap of laughter. Some walked to the mart brought back popcorn hotdogs and tub-sized sodas sat outside in plastic chairs watching the light change. Emergency glances prohibited during mustering service at evening.

The rain unceasing after transport left premises. Earlier at five one muscled window screen off and pushed window back and two stood there considering who should climb in when Welder came along jabbed hand through to release latch. Couldn't think of that, the two saddest in that moment, dying not to go.

After transport vaporized one didn't want to return to own so went to other's instead and noticed how perfectly had left trash packaged evaluation form filled in key placed on top as per orders, everything according to plan except the one who wasn't supposed to be there or to have done that shouting *but we will never see each other again how can you be so* on the bed stared up at ceiling somehow more familiar didn't wake until train whistle sounded hadn't packed kit bag and like all others forced to leave for terrorized deployment.

Rain stopped. Blue fog sucked the air. Free we are to ahoy or destroy any moment *in the dream I eat a bit of your tongue and you eat a bit of mine and we understand each other just fine.*

ON THE BOULEVARD:

One evening many years ago I walked behind you for a few short blocks on Sunset Boulevard and during those moments I experienced a satisfaction more profound than anything I had known with you in your role as responsive and accommodating lover. This is not a complaint. You know well how you excel in that regard. This particular pleasure—which I feel compelled to explain here—came about simply by looking at you as you walked down the street.

A group of us had enjoyed an elaborate meal, had earlier driven down to Los Angeles in mass for the opening of a multi-media theatre event for which my much-admired husband had designed the stage. The evening proceeded nicely, with you and me keeping our electric manifestations to ourselves. This was near the end of our prolonged fading phase and you were almost free of your demon wife and newly engagé with the one true love of your life.

I walked behind you on the bright glitzy boulevard toward the Chateau Marmot where some of us had rooms. Deliberately remaining a few paces behind you, not seeing your face, I was able to observe you for once without regard to the various expectations and disappointments I wore like shackles as a result of how difficult it was to get close to you even more than before.

This night, I had no goal. There were no intimate exchange possibilities looming around a corner. I was happy, for once, walking alone, watching you walking up ahead. You were probably thinking about your new love who had stayed behind to finish a commission. You were missing her, wishing she were with you now. You most certainly were not thinking of me. I was free. The night air bloomed with moist mangled sweetness and I relaxed into an uncanny mood.

I kept my eyes fixed upon you resulting in what I can only describe as a revelation. Like helium balloons let go at a funeral, I was suddenly released from scalding desire and clenched-fist longing. I kept my eyes fixed upon you observing your odd bodily vigor your goofy grace and strength. I wanted nothing from you. Floating.

I watched how you moved in ever-changing curves and angles fluidly along intersecting planes of the henna-lighted street like some cubist drawing or a Mondrian painting: tall, long-limbed, and a bit freakish like me. I sipped, I drank in each nuance of the geometry of your heated awkward presence lumbering along that cracked L.A. sidewalk, receiving a novel pleasure alongside a much needed nascent emotional detachment. I perceived you more clearly than when I clutched and grasped at what I now know must have been a phantom.

You are good at accommodating loved ones. You provide the hook, you fulfill expectations. You know how to please enormously. And yet, I was always—and I don't know why this was true—profoundly dissatisfied. Addiction I guess. I couldn't subsist on the intensity we generated without immediately wanting more. I felt cheated even though it was me doing the leaving most of the time.

What made me so willfully possessive with you? I hadn't been that way before. I expect it's common among a certain type for whom traps are created as appetites are generated. The only sure way to catch a cougar live is to place inside the cage the prey it has just attacked. A romantic, with thwarted instincts, spends her time projecting onto others what she must eventually find in herself.

As you walked, I noticed how the bones of your shoulders carved a twisted trapezoid in space while holding aloft your loosely arranged frame. You wore one of those overlarge jackets, designed for a giraffe, along with a pair of immensely ugly shoes, like armadillos, which made lazy scraping sounds along the rough cement. You added other audibles: sighs, groans, burps, and moans. You jangled the keys in your pocket, dropping a few coins. You laughed at what you were seeing—girls in miniskirts, fishnet stockings, sequined platform shoes, guys with slicked-back hair leaning from convertibles, preening, calling out rudely to the girls.

Hollywood conveyed its ragged, contractual luxuries. We walked the neon-lit street, apart from our noisy group, separated from each other by five or six feet. It was then I began to sense that desire, unsatisfied, might become a tonic or purifying agent. I realized that I hadn't loved you before but had only wanted you in a childish way.

A HILLSIDE:

Above Moraga on the grass in the sun with the moist air and laughter cutting everything into ribbons, jet planes crossing, vultures circling overhead. Death is at hand. Death is banished. Make it run.

Like the spaces inside his atoms, the way the wind rounds the planet, she holds him hard and he is aroused and he rubs himself against her. He does this for long enough that he actually comes inside his jeans as they used to do when they were teens and first in love. These two people are married and have been so for eleven years.

High up on the hills of Moraga, passing through thigh-high grasses, seed-cases singing, clouds floating like bricks in the distance, he wears the leather jacket found underneath a car that hadn't been driven for a decade or more. He's manly, he's rough, he's sweet, kind, intimidating, the boy she married.

She compares, mentally, the atmosphere here with him and other lovers. She knows this is taboo but why stop the thought. It is her job to go wherever it leads. Research, investigation. No fear. There is plenty everywhere for everyone. At least for now. His eyes are wide and deep and very blue pouring all the strength of that sweetness into her. His face more familiar than her own. His mouth closes over hers, he squeezes her breasts inside the fabric. It won't always be like this. Death comes, eventually, having its way with her with him as it did with her mother and then her father's slowly dying scarecrow sorrow.

She wrestles free and flees to the top of the hill surprised to see a shopping mall with automobiles far below. She turns toward a stream with willows bowing, bottom of the embankment, gestures him to follow. She hides behind a large fallen cottonwood with oyster mushrooms blooming along its length.

There was the one who came gloriously, anytime, anywhere, but with a soft tender yearning. There was the one who wanted always to go inside, let me in, he begged, and when she did she knew why. A solid physical merging, piston inside a casing, coalescing the firm with the soft. Entity making. There was the one who gave pleasure wanting nothing for himself... there was...

It is not true that if one examines things clearly an unfavourable comparison will result and a problem will present itself. She has had few lovers and though she brags that she loved each, this one is the only one really that she has ever truly loved. No doubt, in the future, death coming, one or the other will be taken first (unless some kind of miracle occurs as in her dream when they escaped the nuclear attack holding hands and flying off across the bridge in an old Ford Galaxy) and the one left behind will go it alone, move on, get past it, commit suicide, or live on remembering times such as this.

She is a pessimist now, a realist, and it's grand, gets her up in the morning. Being an optimist was too hard, impossible the way things are going. Downhill from here. As a pessimist, things work out better than she could have imagined, because her imagining was so wrong and so clear. You know the game children play, Simon Says, well, she tried to follow orders but was burdened with brains and character and later on, when it was of no use, she got beauty briefly, and lost it and wandered here and there, grateful for everything, except pain of course, though eventually she learned to appreciate even that because it afforded her distance from, yet compassion for, others, all of us losing each moment and everything we cling to after a while. At some point we float wondering: how we got here, who are these people, why is the world so surprising and complete even during hellish times when moments of beauty condense like juniper berries like grains of sand or wheat.

LOLA LEMIRE TOSTEVIN

YESTERDAY, AT YOUR FUNERAL, someone might have whispered in my ear something about the closets of time. He might have said, "She is no longer shut inside the closets of time," but I was so lost in my own thoughts of you that I wasn't sure what he said or what he might have meant. Something perhaps about time closing in or, given your philosophical bent, he might have been referring to a Heideggerian concept of time: "She is no longer shut inside our concepts of time." It would have made more sense.

Still I rather liked the image of time stashed away neatly in a closet in piles of freshly laundered muslin sheets and lace-trimmed pillowcases releasing a subtle scent of lavender. You always did this, added a few drops of lavender to the rinse cycle. To forget was considered an egregious miscalculation on your part and you would restart the cycle over again. Part of you resenting laundry day, part of you insisting it be done the right way. Standing at the ironing board, meticulously ironing and folding sheets that could have done without ironing, the scent of lavender filling the room, the introjection of a gesture that was both scent and symbol. A lock of hair on your forehead brushed back with the back of your hand.

It was the scent of lavender that greeted me when I opened the linen closet after the funeral this morning, a lingering scent of your presence in the orderliness of sheets stacked in neat white blocks with their matching pillowcases beside them. You always held on to a threshold of orderliness, your life justified by detail and commonplace gestures. Like the three large filing cabinets in your study, each one brimming with notes and reflections. The concise deliberations of a meticulous mind. Failed philosopher, you called yourself because you weren't like most philosophers, you didn't spout answers while forgetting the basic questions. The melancholic tribe, you called them. But you, you were never melancholic, not even as you neared the end. Even then, when most people would have given up, you didn't stop questioning. You can't come up with the proper answers if you don't know what to ask, you said, paraphrasing Gertrude Stein on her own deathbed. For you, as for Stein, the answer was already contained in what was being apprehended. Questioning is seeking, you said, and you kept on questioning everything. Your most annoying habit when you were alive, your most touching one now that you are dead.

For one brief moment, while I riffled through your files, time stood still. Literally stood still. You recorded almost everything we talked about over the years, your notes preserving the essence of our talks, sustaining our tête-à-têtes beyond temporal continuity. Our conversations enclosed inside steel cabinets—the same words, same arguments over and over again, the cycle repeating itself. Our lives crystallized in perfect philosophical aphorisms. And for that brief moment, while time stood still, I hated you. You and your rinsing cycles and your notes locked up in your filing cabinets. They seemed so anonymous and distant now, shut up in their closets.

Of time. Was this what your lover said at your funeral? Or was he referring to the concept of time? No matter, I prefer the former. You lived by concepts and I live by images, and a closet is the concrete example of an enclosed space, while a concept can't readily be seen or apprehended. What I need now more than anything are concrete examples I can hold on to. You would have liked this, closet philosopher, shy creature who refused to come out of her shell, trying to get to the heart of things when the heart of everything was right here between us. Or so I thought. I loved you most then.

There was no need for a lover. But you went ahead and questioned our marriage, too. It wasn't enough for you to accept that this was as good as it gets, you spending your days at your desk while I spent mine in my studio until late afternoon when we retreated to the back garden for our daily gin and tonic. Sometimes two. You loved this for a while. Our arguments, our meditations, our ways of existing in which the everyday dominated, the comfort of the accustomed. Everything one and the same and that which would come tomorrow. It reminded you of Heidegger's abandonment of discursive logic, you said. Until one day you announced it was all too much like the old and erroneous concept of space and time moving in a flat line. You needed something different, a different time-line, warped if necessary. You might fall in love again, you said, not admitting that you had already fallen. Hard. The gravity of that falling a force like no other. In view of what we had recently discovered about your illness, what could I say? Oh, I wanted to say plenty. About love. About death. Subjects so utterly exhausted on one hand yet so inexhaustible on the other.

There were two kinds of love, you said, the kind in which you lose yourself and the kind in which you find yourself. In me you'd found yourself, but now you wanted the former. In view of your prognosis, the last thing you needed was to find yourself only to have it all slip away again. Not for you the resigned and graceful, the wise and noble exit. You wanted to lose yourself. Just an affair, you said and it would be silly to give it too much thought, silly and dangerous. So I tried not to think about it. About you and your lover between the lavender-scented sheets. My world stopped then.

Remember the story about the man who asked God to stop the course of the sun, believing this would make time stand still, but time passed even when the sun stood still? This was how I felt. You were right. In the everyday, everything is one and the same and that which will come tomorrow is eternally yesterday's. A closet in which time repeats itself.

When, tonight, I finally lie down for the first time in four days, I will dream of you. I will dream of you, the dream penetrating so deeply that it will reach a region beyond memory and you will be replaced by a time gone by. Tomorrow, when I get up, I will pour out the bottle of lavender and I will wash the linen on the bed and all the sheets and pillowcases in the linen closet. I will break the cycle and time will start anew.

BEVERLEY DAURIO

... prose doesn't exist... there is the alphabet and then there is verse.
... verse is everything, to those who write.
— Mallarmé, quoted in Roberto Calasso, *Literature and the Gods*

[ENVOI
The harshness I mentioned.
This in my defense, trying to make amends.]

ONE
You have no idea who stands welcome in his hat of
bruises, how the precipice of light shines through the
questions you asked.
Slices.

The pale rectangle casts its shadow; a little darkness under the chair expands.

TWO

We want to be so beautiful without paying for it.

We want this hunger without paying for it.

We want tickets to the back lane where glass gives ominous rustling of long black skirts in beige hallways.

Leak of darkness into daylit rooms—to never be afraid again.

We want to know the hidden bridges. The old map or the new, it doesn't matter, only bridges.

THREE

Show me the flashlight again. The new one. How you have to pinch it.

To get light.

Pale hand disturbing cold black water.

Trace notes.

What hope that is, elemental.

FOUR

The questions go in like knives.

Kristeva tells us that poetry replaces human sacrifice. Not a poet, she regards you with precious eyes.

FIVE

Where you entered, corner. Plane, pre-knowledge. Sky bright with winter clouds, telephone poles. Quadrinomial birds, asymptotically altering toward horse shapes against clouds. Opaque shadow of tree, snowy front yard.

Then white wall, black coat on hook. Sweaters and jeans crumpled on the floor.

Huddled and curved.

Naked figures scrawled across blank sheets.

Something "bigger than ourselves."

SIX

If what is hinged, opens.

Traversing, metabolic.

Where you came in, aramaic or rosetta mist, crawling over broken glass, hands hard down and knees, fingers trembling, shivering trust against the gaping hole. Exposed, deep black liquid waves, clawing and formal.

Where you came in, a winter of sex, cats of thought, dogs of memory, loud within frozen buildings; grey, grey, nails hold their windows, nails hold their doors.

Phyla of quotidian breath.

Soft silk repeats anecdotes of stroking arms, elegant cutlery of your hands—standards, rules, small secret legislation at every step. Brutal candour of sunshine vanished behind curtains. The roundness, throbbing and particular, challenges with turning, tiny bare feet over empires of language, the sudden abyss of white between this black and another.

How you would be walking as the water rises. Indigo sleep, and red hunger. Nutrition of bad dreams.

A thousand nails, then: large pink or iron and sharp, pounded.

"The body pays for what you write."

Free of this is seven weeks of terror, twined fingers of two hands gordian and remiss; under the stairs, the butchery or kindness in those boxes you never open, their squareness a simple rebuke, a humiliation.

Where you came in, the lapsing white between four billion figures in their moods and changing, how dense the gathered, layered, ink of us, aching chasms between characters, their drowned and silent shapes across this land of paper, the precipice, these edges.

SEVEN

Truth stands with its hat off.
Annoyed with me.

Tell the truth, then.

Each book you write is an abattoir.

These days are your animals.

GARY BARWIN

THE BUS LETS ME OFF at my stop and I step down onto the warm pavement. I remove my face and, like the sun, I go on, not knowing why. Here is the next day. Pass it on.

Under my face is my other face. It is the same as my first face except that it is secret. I throw it from a cliff-face on the edge of town and it floats like a beast or moving van, snorting and pawing like a chesterfield fluttering toward the sand. Or the birds. For imagine that the sand is all bird, flocks of tiny spherical birds duning as my face falls, birds more ready to believe in sandcastles than in flight.

§

A plot. A pilot. There was a pilot. He swooped. He caught my face in his propellers. He sent my face into the thereafter there shall be no face flying like a pink bird bereft of wings sinking toward the doe-coloured bird-crowded dunes.

§

From the slingshot of the propellers, my face winged through a pre-school window. Sailed over the blocks and biscuits. Knocked off the teacher's glasses and sent the alphabet into a tailspin. Plastered itself, like three sheets in the wind, against Little Roy, cooking plastic food in the miniature kitchen with Becky.

§

HOW LITTLE ROY GOT A NEW FACE

It flew through the window.

§

Little Roy was sent to the Principal's office. Little Roy, what is this new face that you have? Wipe it off. Don't twist it so. You can have another chance. Tomorrow is another day. Today is the day before the first day of the rest of your school year. Unless we suspend you. By your new ears. Out a window or above a cliff.

You're at a crossroads, Roy. A cliffhanger.

§

Meanwhile, inside the chicken, a new plot was hatching.

"It's eggs," Joe says. "Eggs as far as the eye can see. The sun reaches over the horizon, stains the sky yellow."

"You mean we're in some kind of cosmic chicken?" Sue asks.

"And outside of the chicken," Joe says, "who knows what's there? The pale pox of stars on the sky's dark chicken is the limit of our knowledge. We've reached some kind of chicken-event horizon, I mean, except for the feathers. The feathers point to a transcendental metaphysical 'beyond' outside of time. Spacetime runs as if its head has been cut off. It skitters around the yard not knowing when it will end. Or if it has already."

"Is there a farmer?" Betty Sue asks. "What gleeful grasschewing heehaw strawhick in overalls made a spiral galaxy of the neck and then returned to the porch to spit and sip deep of the fizzing amber fossil glow, rocking back and forth on the chair of history? And what star-reflecting axe did he raise and then slam toward the purple jugular of calendar time?"

"And think about it," Joe says, scratching his head. "The chicken of the universe—being relieved of its head and a lot of blood—is quite a bit lighter, and thus gravity is decreased, ergo there are the freebooting feathers of sorrow fluttering through the quintessence, feathers to fill the pillow of regret, the parka of loss, to fletch the arrows of progress. We screw up our one eye, take a deep breath, then release the bowstring, and in the distance the chicken falls," Joes continues. "It's as simple as that. The faceless chicken of being is limp in the dirt and, we're a bit surprised by what we've done, we slump our shoulders and shuffle off to the barn. And after the ateleologic spirograph of the dancing chicken ends in the dust, what do we do with its head or face or beak? Make soup, or a puppet? Maybe hide it in our sock or desk drawer? Perhaps prank the bus driver when he's not looking, slide the head into his thermos, or mail it to an unwitting grade school class?" Joe shrugs and presses down on the gas pedal. He and Becky Sue speed towards the furniture-repair store, passing the graveyard, the beer store, the salmon haberdashery, and the hotdog stand of Little Roy's dad, finally released from the hatchery of grad school and all those eggshells.

§

Meanwhile, there's Roy's new face itself, hanging on a narrative cliff. Little Roy, the alphabet block technician, the virtuoso of the plastic kitchen and the wincing eyes now filled with tears and currently in the office of Vanderbilt the Vice-Principal, whipping his dark cape over Roy's cowering and miniature face like a storm-clouded sky. The face looks through the window and hopes to fly with or without the rest of Roy as a corpo-real tailfin. A face seeking freedom in the yellow yolk of sunshine.

The Vice-Principal gathers his cape, adjusts his mask. I have become two men and so have earned the right to this Batman face, he says. One day I was Ira Vanderbilt, grade-seven boy, third-string member of the Recycling Club; the next I was a bat huge as the darkness of night. I stamp my foot on the stage at assemblies and students gasp open-mouthed for I am the sum of their shadows. Little Roy, this new face of yours does not belong in school. It is not of this earth, of this time, of this school district. It must be surrendered. Fold it as if it were a paper airplane or the wings of a pink bat. I will open the cloudless doors of my storage closet and find a shelf on which to give it a home. For here are the faces of the Middle Ages, of the Renaissance, of a fellow who once thought he was God. Here are the glove-like mugs of Randy the Caretaker, of Donna the Librarian, of Freddy the Monkey King, of Mrs. Filomena's grade-three French immersion class. Today is the first day, Little Roy. There is dust on the face of the earth. There is darkness behind your new face, behind the insolent crater of your smile. You will remove your face and place it on a blond shelf in this closet for all time. Your bones have the whiteness and shimmer of distant stars pulled by an expanding schoolhouse. Soon time will cease to exist. There will be nothing but this closet of faces, here in my Vice-Principal's office. Around its locked doors, its taupe exterior, time will whisper its whirlwind no more. I will be free to be a Batman on the deckchair of my destiny. I will BBQ my life, make it pure with fire. Your face is a swallow flying for but a moment through the third-grade classroom of time. Outside, darkness, storm, endless fields of incomplete homework and the forgotten inhalations of schoolchildren gasping at the translucent chickenskin of the known universe. One day you're a mouse. The next a dresser drawer. A nuclear explosion, a neglected story, a cliffhanger, then a bus driver's thermos lost somewhere in the meanwhile.

STEVEN ROSS SMITH

who

in this

shadow quadrant

is gasping, who

underneath

glimmers up, glimmers up, glimmers up

— Paul Celan★

§

ONE ISLAND MORNING

SOON. IN THE distance, a siren will wail.

§

BLANCHE

The lean, frail woman clutches the railing and works her way down the stone steps beside her house, toward her swimming pool. She's bent forward. Her knuckles are bony and white. Beads of sweat break out on her forehead, wilting the bangs of her gray hair to hang flat and limp. Her arms shake as she uses all her strength to hold herself up and edge one foot at a time, reaching toward each next and lower step. She relies on, and fights, the pull of gravity. The pain in her deteriorating spine feeds her body's wish to crumble.

"Goddam! Come on Blanche," she wills herself.

A cool slight breeze buffets the early morning air, light just breaking through the trees. Blanche shakes and shivers at the same time. Her bright red robe clings or folds open in the wind's flutter and in her struggle. Her nightdress, glimpsed beneath, is pale green, thinning with age.

In her concentration it seems as if the whole world, all of her life, closes in, becomes only the few square feet her body occupies, and the push to get her right foot to move a few inches. Just one more step to be close enough to reach for the walker.

She urges her foot forward, but something inside her resists—her body at war with itself and her will. Time has brought her this.

She's tiring. When the foot moves over the edge of the step, her leg will be hung in space and all her weight will be poised on the left leg—will it hold? Perspiration and tears merge at the corners of her eyes. She grits her teeth against her fear and quavering.

Toes, then her foot's arch, and finally her heel move past the lip of the step. Momentum is gained, then gives.

Forward Blanche lurches, plunging, crumpling, reaching. She feels in slow motion. Time dashes, time brakes, in one tremulous moment. Time batters her bones.

§

KATE

"I'll get those fuckers. I'll get them out of here."

Among the trees, night's dimness lifts slowly in the dawn. Kate moves like a shadow, but deliberately.

"This is mine, my sanctuary, my place to escape that sonofabitch." Did she speak these words or did they flash like a familiar headline in her mind? She pauses and listens but there is no trace or echo of her voice in the air. Her face is pale, her eyes dark.

Kate holds the red and black can with both hands, squirts barbeque fluid on the pile of wood scraps—plywood triangles, short ends and shavings—by the corner of the building. It's the skeleton of a cabin, with standing timber and crossbeams, milled from trees felled to make this clearing. Window and door frames are roughed in, plywood floor laid. The structure and the pile of scrap is not far from the camping trailer and close to the stack of lumber waiting to be applied as siding and finishing boards. She turns and fires a few squirts in the direction of the stack, careful not to splash her black runners or gray pants.

She hums softly, a flat indiscernible melody, but with determination. So absorbed is she, that the soft hooting of the owl in the nearby stand of spruce goes unnoticed. But a car scooting up the gravel road at the end of the long driveway causes her to stop, to stand stock still until she is sure the sound is receding.

Turning back and aiming higher, she sprays a blast of fluid directly onto an upright support post.

"Hmmmmm-mmm," Kate hums, but now there is an attitude of reverence. In her skin she can already feel the familiarity of fire, its inviting warmth, the thrill of its gyrations. She reaches into her bag, slips the fluid container in, and pulls out a yellow butane igniter. She clicks its trigger until a small shaft of flame, orange and blue, pops out the end of the short black barrel.

Her humming stops, the soft hiss of the lighter her new music. She watches it, listens, then licks her finger, passes it through the flame.

"Now to turn back the clock," she whispers. "Goodbye to your sawing and hammering, all your fuckin' noise."

She lowers the igniter toward the wood scraps. There's a *whoosh* and a ball of orange flame.

She backs away, watching to make sure the fire takes well, then turns and walks slowly up the grade, pausing now and again to look back. The flames lick their red and orange tongues, hungry and bright, upward from the ground, enveloping the beam, illuminating the clearing, as if to rush the dawn. Kate fades into the forest's shadows and disappears.

§

BERNARD AND TINA

On the cabin porch, Bernard sits, leaning on the hard pale tabletop. He likes to watch the dawn in the forest, away from technology and distraction. Sun begins to peek through the silhouetted trees. In the play of light and shadow, sunbeams lift foliage here and there into distinct visibility—the maple's autumn-yellow leaves, the cedar with its flat green needles.

He hears the car brake in the turnaround, the engine shut off and the car door slam. Tina walks up the driveway past the perky salal bush.

"There's no use," Tina says. "She said *stay away*, and slammed the door." Tina disappears behind the thick tree trunk. Her words droop in the air.

With the sun's movement, the light shifts to the bark of the towering tree Bernard calls *precipitous fir* because of its sky-reaching height and its off-kilter lean. In a crevasse in the aged tree's scaly bark, a ray spotlights an insect wing caught and fluttering, as if given a second life. A raven croaks somewhere overhead.

"That's unfortunate... very sad." Bernard aims his words in the direction of the tree, continues, "She's shocked. She'll come around."

A tear glints on Tina's cheek as she comes into view.

"How soon?" she asks.

"Can't say... eventually, I guess."

"She's my daughter. I can't wait that long."

Bernard is aware of the pressure of his elbow on the table, his temple resting on his fist, his wrist cocked, forearm straight and transmitting the weight. His shoulders ache from yesterday's wood chopping. He shifts.

Tina's footsteps crunch on the underlay of sand and stone, seeds and cones.

Bernard has been trying to determine if the old tree is a Douglas or a Grand fir. Not so easy for the untrained eye. It has not been important until recently. And now in his hand, a cone dropped from one of the branches three or four stories above his head reveals the tell-tale mouse tail peeking out from under the cone's scales; or as it says in the field guide on the table: *the three-forked bracts resembling a mouse's feet and tail.*

"It's a Douglas," he says, as Tina disappears around the corner of the cabin. He hears the door open and close, her footsteps moving closer, until she walks through the open screen doorway to the porch to sit opposite him at the table. Her hair is auburn and tousled, her brow furrowed. Her gaze looks not outward, but in.

"I thought when she and I found each other everything would be okay," Tina says.

"There's been that thirty-three-year gap," Bernard replies, straightening up and stretching his hands over his head, flexing his shoulders. "Lotta water under the..."

"And she's furious at me for that, for letting her go. But I was a teenager. I was unfit."

"You shouldn't..." begins Bernard.

Tina interrupts again. "I wish I could go back, fix what happened then."

"How could you? What you did was best." He reaches his fingers across the table to rest on the back of her hand.

A sudden breeze comes down the slope behind them, as if sneaking up, and despite their distraction, its swoosh and pulse catches their ears and carries their gaze to the sway of the tall trees and the shuddering leaves. Bernard adjusts his reading glasses, peers over top of them.

"Do you ever think about this tree here, the Douglas fir?" he asks, tilting his head in the tree's direction.

"Just about whether it might fall on us. Might be a good thing."

"It won't do that, it's our guardian."

"How do you know?"

"Look at it—this old tree, its patience. Standing, growing, waiting, even breathing for us, and doing it all so slowly, with such majesty."

"Screw the sappy metaphor. Next you'll be hugging that tree... instead of me."

"Tina, she'll come around. Don't push. Give her time." Bernard rises, moves toward Tina, and with his arms embraces her deep sadness.

"Stop! Stop! It's now!!" Honey, stiffening, breathless, in the seat beside him.

Dean pulls onto the edge of the narrow road, the grass just beginning to lighten in the dawn. Honey's head tilts back on the headrest, her throat is white. He can see her pulse, rapid in a vein.

"Shit," Dean says, "what'll I do?"

"Help me." Her knees pulsing in and out.

"Can you hang in until we get there?"

A low moan from deep in her chest; head side to side.

Dean leaps from the driver's seat, runs behind the truck, pulls a blue tarp from the box, jumps over the ditch and spreads it on the narrow strip of grass between the ditch and fence.

"Here," he says, taking her under her arms and guiding. He helps her ease down onto the tarp, runs back to the truck, reaches in toward the steering wheel, honks the horn madly.

Honey twists, her body locking and releasing as her back arches. Her fair shiny hair spreads, a writhing halo about her head; her fingers clutch the tarpaulin.

Dean rushes back to her side. Her skirt is up over her knees, her legs splayed.

"Pull my panties off," she gasps, "it's... it's... "

He pulls at her underwear but catches it on her sandal. With a yank, shoes and underthings come off, are thrown to the side. Dean runs back to the truck to honk some more. Then back to her.

"Okay, I'm with you, Hon," Dean kneels, panting.

They hadn't planned it this way—well not *any* way. But it was a glorious night that led to this. Celebrating their first year of dating with wine and crackers and brie at the beach under the wide arc of stars, and no one else there; the gentle, constant push of the ocean onto the sand and stones creating a crystalline melody. Snuggling into two sleeping bags zipped together, they cuddled, clutched, stroked and gasped, gushed giggles, laughter and tears, on the thin strand between the trees, the sky, the salty sea. They hung on a thread, the thin miraculous fibre of human existence and communion. And the life lines that were each of them became deeply entwined in finger traces, tongue caresses, pulses of skin surfaces, moving as one. That night on the cusp of eternity the universe sang through their bodies. They changed the course of history—at least, their own.

This morning that universe has narrowed to a square of tarpaulin and Honey's shining, globular belly, her body's firing up, its spasms and contractions readying to deliver new life.

Dean's pulse races, his hands are uncertain, his mind a dazzle of confusion, but he's enraptured by Honey's beauty, and her pain. He runs his fingers through his sleep-ruffled hair.

A car pulls up. Dean recognizes Bernard, a neighbour.

"What's up?" Bernard looks from Dean to Honey, says "Honey," and nods, cordial despite the circumstances.

"Her water broke early. The first one is coming now!" says Dean.

"You call the doctor?"

"The cellphone won't connect. We thought we could make it."

Bernard kneels beside Dean. He speaks rapidly. "You said the first one, right? Twins, right? I'll get the doc, okay?"

"Hurry."

Bernard rushes to his car and peals away.

"You okay, Honey?" Dean tries to sound comforting. His heart thuds against his ribs, pounds with the moment's impossibility, its wonder.

"Uh-huh," she says exhaling, her mouth widening. Dean looks at her face. An intense energy—strained and courageous—that Dean's not seen before pulses from her cheeks, her eyes, her forehead. His left hand waits between her legs; he reaches the other to rub her belly.

"Take a deep breath... gently... the baby's coming. I'm here. Lots of time. We'll be fine." His waiting hand shakes.

Honey nods, emits a small smile, and begins to breathe slow and deep, her whole body tuning its attention toward the birthings.

§

BLANCHE

A shaft of pain shoots through Blanche's hip, the corner of the step digging in. Her arms angle up, as in her crumpling—her pelvis and knees giving out at the same time—she'd managed to grab the rail and land on her backside. She feels in a cold sweat and can see the cloth of her robe quiver with her trembling. Her face ashen white. Sweat rolls down her cheeks, collects in the creases of her neck.

"Nghghghmn." She sighs and moans, letting the pain escape from her chest and lips like a puff of wind in a veil. Her world spins. She stays sitting until her head clears and the shaking stops.

She sees blood on her knuckle. Her housecoat and nightie are pushed up, revealing her sagging thighs.

"Damn! What now?" she wonders. She remembers how she used to bound down these stairs, swim lengths every morning, year after year, right here in this pool. But no longer.

A feeble "help" feathers from her throat as if uttered by someone else. Then silence. A deep breath to the bottom of her pain makes her wince, stirs her determination.

"Today is not for frailty," she whispers.

The water of the pool is still but for a slight chuff across its surface where the breeze buffs it. Here and there gleam a few rays of sunlight. The sea-blue liner of the pool absorbs both the light and the darkness, making it seem as if there is no limit beneath the surface, making it look like a sky or a bottomless opening to another dimension.

The water's glimmer appears to be winks and nods, beckoning. *Come on. Come Blanche. You can make it,* calling her to slip into the water and be eased of her body's weight.

She pushes with her arms, pulls with her heels, slides her hips bit by bit toward the calling water, its promise. Its promise of release.

§

THE SIREN

In the distance the wail of the siren calls the volunteer firefighters and medics into action. The wail rolls across the island's hills and meadows, up the steep slopes toward the sky, down toward the streams and low-lying swamps. It rolls along the paved and gravel roadways, nudges through trees and scrambles over rocks, moving outward, uniting everyone on the island through their ears. Everyone stops for that brief moment to look off, eyes tilted slightly upward, concerned, wondering. Everyone strains to hear the real message of the whining siren, a message singular and without embellishment. Yet to every pair of ears, the siren brings a reminder of mortality, a brush with disaster, the knowledge that something close and unfortunate is unfolding, and that next time it could be for them. Then comes the long silence that builds with the siren's fade. But soon into it jabs a car engine starting up, or truck tires speeding along a gravel road, or a shout that echoes. Everyone is thinking "I hope," and the thought fills with their own concerns and wishes for the safety or protection of someone or something, for a bit more time, for a normal, or even an extraordinary day.

§

* From *Selected Poems and Prose of Paul Celan*, by Paul Celan, translated by John Felstiner. Copyright © 2001 by John Felstiner. Used by permission of W.W. Norton & Company, Inc.

JOHN SHIRLEY

HE STOOD AT THE WINDOW. looking out at the gray afternoon; the chill sea stretched out, waiting with vast, cold assurance below his cliffside house.

Grigsby had managed not to go to the locked closet for three weeks. He did drugs, he got drunk, he gambled, he chased women. It kept him away from the closet. He knew full well these things were vices; he knew it wasn't good for him to distract himself that way. But he reasoned that it was better than opening the closet.

Now, standing by the window, his back to the closet—but feeling its pull, which was surely, oh most definitely just in his imagination—he thought about destroying the machine locked within it. But he didn't move; he didn't go to the tool shed for the sledge hammer. He simply stood looking out the window. It was winter in British Columbia, and the sea, constrained by the rocky islands of the Sound, shrugged its chill gray body restlessly, thrashing to white spume against the rocks. Very cold, that water would be. Very cold.

Perhaps he could go somewhere else. Somewhere earlier. But it always happened that he merged with his earlier self, remembering where he'd come from—remembering the future—but able to make only minor changes in the past. So he'd be drawn as if through a sluice to that spring day overlooking Anvil Rock, though it took years to get there.

Perhaps he might perfect the machine, and go elsewhere... before his birth. Or to go somewhere after his death. But...

But it called to him now.

Try again. This time you can save her. This time...

Strange phrase, that, 'this time.' In view of what he'd learned. "'This time,'" Grigsby murmured. "*This* time. This time."

The phone rang. Stopped ringing. Rang again. Stopped ringing. Rang again. Again, again.

It was Sanguelo, of course. He was always very insistent. He would want clarity on the new mine in Santo Miguel. He would want to know if the proper Brazilian authorities had been bribed. Ring. He would want to know if Grigsby planned to supervise the open-pit mine himself. Ring, ring. If the gold assay was indeed confirmed. Ring, ring, ring. If their legal problems had been dealt with...

"Go the hell away!" Grigsby shouted, never turning from the window; his voice rattling the glass.

As if chastened, the phone stopped ringing.

Grigsby snorted. "First time he's..." His voice trailed off. He gazed out the window.

The key in his pocket seemed to press against his hip. The key to the closet.

Grigsby felt the shift inside him that meant he was going to give in. He wasn't going to go to Vancouver to find women, to take drugs, to throw money at a card table; to feel himself slowly burning away, like a slow fuse. No. He was going to do something worse. It was worse because it seemed hopeless. Maddeningly hopeless. Because it meant reliving that day.

He was sorry he'd ever funded Kosinksi's research. *"I can take your consciousness back in time. It remains to be seen if your body can go..."*

Anybody else would have sent the scientist packing, after mad-sounding remarks of that kind. Many had, in fact—Kosinski had already tried over a hundred possible funders. Grigsby had been a longshot—he was interested in funding research into mine engineering, not quantum theory, not time travel. But Kosinski was his wife's nephew, and he was sentimental about her memory, so...he'd given him some money to work with. And then, a year later, it had happened, and he'd gone desperately to Kosinski, and then...

Who knew?

He should have shot the bastard, not paid him. But maybe this time...

He sighed, and turned away from the window, walked across the empty room to the closet, and unlocked it. Inside was...

§

"Hey Dad! Are we going or not!"

Grigsby looked up from his PC to see his daughter, Maria, smiling nervously at him from the doorway. She was an earnest, deeply tanned graduate student—very nearly always, as now, in jeans and work-shirt—with her mother's long wavy black hair and her father's blue eyes; and now she had that 'There's something I want to talk to you about' look. She liked to have these talks, always about something she regarded as deeply serious and epochal, in fine restaurants, or on the beach, or in the back of a cathedral, someplace that seemed to impart drama to the discussion. Today it was a walk along the cliffs near his sprawling house.

It would be her house, one day, he thought. She was his only child and her mother was five years in the grave. If she would just wait for her time—let him be himself while she waited—

"Coming, Dad?"

"You bet. We taking a lunch?"

"No, I'm going to make lunch for you on the deck, after. It's a beautiful day..."

He looked wistfully at his email. Jose Sanguelo had a very urgent tone—was quite disturbed about the bad publicity, the sudden judicial interference in Grigsby Gold Mines Ltd., when all had been so sweetly copasetic with the Brazilian authorities for so many years. Still, it would keep for an hour or so.

He stood and looked for his coat—and then saw that she was holding it out to him, smiling.

§

Yellow crocuses were blooming along the cliff path, waving in the wind amidst new grass. The grass had a fresh greenness, that seemed the very colour of innocence. The breakers below were cottony white in the spring sunshine, almost the same colour as the few wispy clouds in the turquoise sky. A brisk wind whipped their hair, it was true, but there was nearly always a wind here.

"You still seeing that lawyer kid?" he asked her.

His daughter laughed and shook her head. "Oh, my God, if he could hear you call him a lawyer kid. He's thirty-one."

"Just seems boyish to me, I guess. More like just out of college."

"Because he's an idealist?"

"There's being an idealist and then there's being silly. He always pushes everything too far."

"Well... he doesn't, Dad. I mean... I met him when he was working with Amnesty International, in Sao Paulo—they're very established and serious. They're not some flaky organization. The UN respects them."

"Yeah, well, I don't respect the UN either. What was it you wanted to talk to me about? You had that earnest carrying-the-world-on-your-shoulders look."

She scowled. That face-transfiguring scowl she'd inherited from her mom. From pretty to ridiculous in a split second. "It's pretty serious, Dad." She dropped the scowl and stopped at the peak of the cliff, turning to gaze at him, hair whipping around her face. She brushed a few strands from her eyes, squinting in the bright sunlight. "What I carry on my shoulders is my karma—you've paid for everything I have with blood money."

He stared at her. She'd tasked him about his mines before but never so self-righteously, so bluntly. "So— would you like to repay me the college funds? Like me to take away the annuity?"

"I won't be taking the annuity any more, actually. And you may need the money, for your own lawyers. Dad—" Maria made a sound that was something close to a moan. "I had to help Joel when he—he's representing the Santos family."

He felt like he'd been struck by a baseball bat. "Your fiancé is representing the people who're suing me?"

"The Santos brothers have moved to Vancouver. And..." She licked her lips. "I think I'm getting chapped up here. Maybe we should go in the house."

"No! Just stay right there and tell me exactly what you mean by you had to 'help' him!"

"I... copied some of your files. The money transfers to Colonel Vega. Dad, you paid those soldiers to *murder* those people so they'd stop talking about the cyanide from the mine—so they'd keep quiet about your company poisoning the village. What was I going to do? I... look, you're my dad and I love you. I didn't want to just... screw you over, even for a good cause, from a... like, from a distance. I wanted to tell you face to face what I'd done. I think you should own up to it and... pay restitution. I mean, up here, you're not likely to be prosecuted for hiring—"

"I didn't hire anybody to kill anyone *anywhere*!"

Of course it was a lie. But he had learned that lies work best when you're deeply insistent, over and over. And he was never going to cop to having anyone killed—especially not to Maria.

"Dad—I know what you did. You were sloppy about the emails. We have the money trail. You paid to kill those people to keep them quiet. And... it has to end. I mean, Joel told me about it and I... couldn't believe it. I thought of you as tough and conservative and even ruthless but— not without human feelings. I figure you managed to...to forget they were people too, for awhile. I *know* you have human feelings, Dad. You were good to me and Mom. Mostly. But..."

"So Joel poisoned your mind!" (Why was he saying that, again? This time... he must remember. The closet. The closet. The future. He must... but it was so hard to believe it, so hard to...)

"Dad—should we go over the paperwork? You made me an officer in the company and I... on that authority I gave it to the prosecutor. Now, like I said, he won't be able to—"

"You gave... you let that boy tell you what to think and you turned your own father in... you...." (No! This time he... but he felt so caught up, so angry...) "You treacherous little bitch! I'm already under investigation for taxes—" All the blue had sucked out of the sky—it seemed white now, with veins of red. The sea seemed to roar in fury—in demand. The wind whined in pity for him—stabbed in the back by his own child... a child he had given everything to!

"I didn't know that you were under—"

"And now you're going to help them destroy me! You already *have*!" (This time, remember—the closet— but the feeling was so strong, so...)

"Dad—it has to stop! It's a matter of conscience! Someone has to—to stop people like you! I'm so ashamed of our family, of the way we live, of—"

That was what did it. *Ashamed of our family.*

He lashed out, backhanded her, and she staggered for a moment, teetered, and there was a second when he might have, might have, might have caught her. (Now! Remember! The closet, you—)

But then Maria was falling backwards over the cliff, screaming. Falling, falling. Striking Anvil Rock below...And he was looking over the edge, wanting to throw himself after her, but not having the courage.

Seeing the dark red splash around her head, below, diluting to pink when the wave washed over her...

Then the machine in the closet detected the 'moment of return' setting and he was caught up in a vortex, screaming, twisting...stopping.

Swaying in the dusty closet. Sobbing in the darkness.

He fumbled for the door, opened it, stepped blinking out into the room, with only moments having passed from the time he'd entered the closet. The winter light came pale through the window of the barren room; the room that had been Maria's bedroom.

He closed the closet door behind him and went to the window.

How many times is that? he asked himself. He thought about it. *How many times have I gone back?*

At least three hundred.

Next time. Next time, the three-hundred-and-first time.

Next time, he wouldn't kill her.

MICHAEL DEAN

I WAS FIVE YEARS OLD. I was locked in the total darkness of the closet in my parents' bedroom. I was listening to screams in the dark as my brother, locked in the closet with me, pounded on the door and yelled to our mother, begging to let us out. My brother and I were locked in the closet in the middle of the afternoon having hidden there to jump out and surprise our mother when she got back from the corner store. This was my brother's idea. He was two years older than me and full of ideas. However, when we got into the closet neither of us noticed that the doorknob on the inside of the closet door didn't work, that it just spun around when you turned it. No one else had noticed this problem either. Who needs to unlock a closet door from the inside? As my brother screamed and pounded on the door, I stood unable to act, twitching and sweating in the dark, thinking I was going to faint. Then I found myself sitting on the floor in the total darkness reaching for a shoebox at the back of the closet under what was now a pile of shoes, opening the shoebox and taking out what I already knew was one of my father's paperback mysteries that my mother made him keep there because of their lurid covers. The shoebox was the secret hiding place of my parents' private bedroom things, my brother having revealed it to me just the week before on Saturday night, when we were supposed to be in bed, our parents out dancing and the babysitter listening to *Inner Sanctum* on the radio in the kitchen with the lights out.

I sat on the floor of the closet holding my father's paperback. I didn't know how to read, but I knew that reading would calm me. I did what I had watched my mother do every day in the quiet of the afternoon and in the evening after dinner: I held the book in such a way that my elbows were bent enough to bring the text to what felt a comfortable distance from my eyes. I shifted the book from one hand to the other. I bent the book back to stretch the binding. I ran my thumb and index finger down the edge of the page and turned the page briskly, always turning just one page at a time. My mother read that way, and I held my father's book the same way and read the invisible text while my brother screamed and threw his body against the closet door.

That's how I learned to read: sitting in the dark. I felt none of my brother's desperation and panic. I remember only a sensation of drifting as if in a rapture, as if in a boat rocking on a lake while fishing, which I had done with my father and brother in the summer, in the morning in the reeds in the marsh on the shores of Lake Scugog.

At the same moment that I was having this experience of rapture in the closet, my brother and I were about to be rescued by the same boy who listened to *Inner Sanctum* on our kitchen radio in the dark and who lived next door and was thirteen. His name was Billy Snooks, and after he rescued us he went home and told his mother: "When Mrs Dean goes shopping she locks her children in the closet."

I learned two things about myself from the experience of reading in the dark while being locked in the closet: I am subject to anxiety attacks due to claustrophobia, and I am capable of rapture as a means of screening these states. Over the years I have experienced the same rapture, usually when reading, but also when listening to music or looking at art. I learned a third thing from my closet experience, but I didn't learn it until recently: I learned that I had become skilful not only at using rapture to relieve myself of unbearable feeling states, but I developed a preference for rapture over all other feeling states. I learned this last week while lying in bed with my wife before going to sleep, leafing through a book of the frescoes of Renaissance painter Fra Angelico. In his fresco of *The Annunciation*, (in which the angel Gabriel announces to Our Lady that she is pregnant with God's child), Fra Angelico depicts Our

Lady as being interrupted at her reading by the angel, and in her surprise she tips her book forward so the viewer sees that the text is blank. As I looked at this fresco, I realized that Fra Angelico was depicting Our Lady having the same experience of rapture that I had had while reading in the dark in the closet of my parents' bedroom, and realized that Fra Angelico was suggesting that the blankness of the text I read in the closet was not unique, that blankness is fundamental to the nature of all text. This led, of course, to the obvious conclusion that the blankness of Our Lady's text was the same blankness as in the text I held in my hands in the darkness of my parents' closet when I was five. In other words, the book I held in my hands as I waited for my mother's return from the corner store was the same book as the one Our Lady held in her hands as she waited for the angel to tell her she was with child.

However, this raises the question: if text is blank by nature, then what is narrative? Let me answer this question by returning to my parents' bedroom. The book I read while locked in my parents' closet was one of my father's detective novels that my mother made him keep in their private shoebox because of the overly suggestive covers. As I mentioned earlier, my brother had showed me the shoebox a week before we locked ourselves in the bedroom closet. Inside the shoebox we had seen various feminine products of my mother's, along with my father's pocketbooks, and condoms and spermicidal cream. The shoebox was burgundy-coloured and sat on the floor at the back of the closet along with other shoeboxes and my mother's off-season shoes. The picture on the cover of my father's detective novel was that of the dead body of a woman, lying on the floor next to a bed, wearing only a black slip and one black nylon. A pair of black high-heeled shoes was beside the bed partly draped by other articles of lingerie that surely slipped from the bed during the death struggle. *Love Is Murder,* the title says, in red diagonally across the cover.

Evidently, by its very nature, text generates two narratives. We can see, in the case of my father's detective novel, that the obvious narrative involves the dead body of a woman, while the hidden narrative—the one that arose in the mind of a five-year-old reader encountering the novel as a blank text—the narrative is one of drifting in a boat with his father and brother, which can be seen as a screen against his intolerable experience of anxiety and panic on finding himself locked in a closet separated from his mother.

I should also mention that on the night my brother and I rifled through my parents' shoebox and looked at the cover of *Love Is Murder,* my brother pointed to the body of the dead woman and said: "Do you know who that is?"

It was obvious to me it was our mother, but my brother said: "That's the reader. That's how you end up if you read this book."

"Dead," I said.

"Yes," my brother nodded. "Murdered."

Although my brother was seven then and knew how to read, my recent experience with Fra Angelico's frescoes, which taught me that blank text is universal, suggests that while my brother wasn't *wrong* exactly about the reader being the murder victim, his understanding falls short of including the idea that the reader is also the one who gives birth to the narrative through the act of reading, the narrative being the story that arises from the reader's blank mind.

All my life I have lived haunted by my inability to come to terms with some unbearable feeling state, as if I'd witnessed something horrible through a keyhole in a closet door, a murder that took place while black lingerie gathered in a pool of its own slipperiness around the murder victim's high-heeled shoes, and my breathing grew quicker and more shallow, sitting down in a rapture in a darkened closet with a burgundy shoebox open in front of me, my hands holding a book at a comfortable distance from my eyes as if I can see anything, as if I can read, as if I understand narrative, as if I know whether I'm the writer or the reader. I wonder, too, maybe, after all, if I'm just a minor element within the narrative. Am I the spinning doorknob? Or the missing black nylon? Or the missing word for the missing black nylon, that is, the word *stocking*?

I can see that my problem has been one of confusing the two levels of narrative, not knowing if I am looking at the murder of my mother through a keyhole, or viewing the cover of a detective novel in a shoebox.

What about the blankness of the text in Fra Angelico's *Annunciation*? Would you say, dear reader, that this is a message to the viewer that the painting must be read as a screened narrative that covers a deeper narrative containing the memory of the night the painter witnessed the primal scene between his parents, their sexual union, perhaps on the night they conceived the painter's younger brother? Or would you say that Fra Angelico was not confusing the two levels of narrative the way I had, but was instead integrating them? In other words, the blank text held by Our Lady in *The Annunciation* must be taken as an indication that Fra Angelico understands that blankness occurs naturally at the heart of human experience and that this blankness is to be endured so we can see beyond the narrative to the text beneath that waits for us. In this view, Fra Angelico is not afraid of the text. He is not anxious about his feeling state.

We could conclude that in *The Annunciation* we see what happens when the reader waits a long time, and patiently, for the true narrative to be revealed to him. Therefore, in the painting we see the reader at the exact moment he experiences the end of waiting, as the true narrative arises from out of the blank text in the form of an angel who rescues him from blankness, the reader finding himself holding his dream in his hands, tipping this dream forward and announcing to the world that the waiting is over for all of us, our time is nigh, our womb is blessed. So, dear reader, it's only a matter of time now for you and me, as we wait inside this narrative together, to be let out. I yell and throw myself against the door; you hold the book, elbows bent, eyes focused. Who generates the narrative? Who needs to unlock a closet door from the inside?

KARL JIRGENS

NOW, THE WARM AUTUMN RAINS have begun, and yellow leaves sweep about my feet as I walk to work. Lately, she's been sending me on-line links to kink pages. Research for a new book. Leather bound, corsets, harnesses, halters, for her, or him, as well as latex and PVC, all tastefully illustrated with attractive models, busty, long-legged women, lean, muscular men. Toying with mischief. Enticing, the way it was that summer night. Yesterday it was nurse and doctor outfits, naughty patient gowns. Stockings, hose, and thigh-high fishnets, vintage-style replicas of the forties with the back-seam, garter belts, and naughty illustrations from the days after the Second World War. Eisenhower vintage. She sends them to my work email which I find mildly embarrassing but secretly stimulating. Restraints, braces, dungeons in a box, all shipping details accompanied by friendly looking receptionists, actually actors or actresses in costume, players playing, purportedly ready to respond immediately to your phone call or internet order. Adult services. I flip to other emails, try to be discreet when my secretary walks in to drop off mail or documents for signature. Or, I forward the messages accompanied with her coy comments to my private email where I can consider them and the websites in greater leisure and privacy. I recall that midsummer night. She said, "Just because we're going to your place for a drink doesn't mean anything will happen." I agreed and had no reason to think otherwise, but was intrigued. We talked politics, poetics, drank wine. I've moved since then, to another house. My short-term lease was up in the summer home. I had hoped to find something more permanent by summer's end. Instead, I now find myself bouncing from place to place. Nomadic. In transition. Searching. It was only a couple days after the encounter when I received an electronic message:

> *Lost: Bangle-style with simple face, contemporary ladies' watch. Open links on either side of face and smaller links on underside. Adjustable. Face, mother-of-pearl accented with gold hands and markers complementing polished gold-tone case and bracelet. Scratch-resistant crystal. Water resistant to thirty metres. Jewellery-style clasp. Sentimental value. Reward if found.*

I remember the moment. Her sudden decision to take it off. The abandon and relief. "I'm taking this watch off.

Hmph." I find that I can situate myself in that moment. I am there, near her, watching her hand place it on a nearby ledge. I seem to remember a ledge being above my head at the time. But, I could be wrong. I was, we were intoxicated, by each other, wine, poetics, casting a net of words arching from Yeats to Olson, a wide net stretching from the early myths to Graves counting the slow heartbeats and the bleeding-to-death of time, Eliot and what the thunder said, and Edward Lear, the blues, the Beats, the roxy music of passion, dissonance, the moan of doves in immemorial elms, even Tennyson, when the blood creeps and the nerves prick, when time is a maniac scattering dust, or life a fury slinging flame, and we spoke of Bishop's September rain and what we planned when summer changed to autumn with the iron kettle singing on the stove, and Stein's roses, and Stein's roses. The art of Picasso, cubist constructions, and his African influence. The night was hot and words steamed around epics, vengeful gods, mornings after, the jouis-sance of Handel's royal fireworks, Huxley and his doors of perception lighting our fires. Diviners and divinations. I-Ching, Tarot and what the cards said. At one point, half-attentively, I watched her open the link and thrust her watch on a ledge. The ledge seemed higher at the time, but perhaps I only thought that because I was not standing. I can't remember precisely. I think I was lying down, but near. I can't remember exactly when the watch came off. We were talking, sitting on the couch,

THE CLOSETS OF TIME

drinking Fat Bastard. Talking books, periodicals. Cards on the table. At some point, we kissed. I am there now, in thought, and it is earlier, perhaps later, or both, and we are standing at the fridge pouring wine into glasses. Talking dreams, and she's telling me I'm talking to her head, not her body, taking her seriously, radical poetics, muses and writing, we draw arcs of thought in the midnight air, she digs I'm talking to her head, it arouses her, in her loins she says, and she likes the wine, too. Debating metaphor as opposed to accumulation. Bodies, tongues in motion. An undefined time later, was it back at the couch, my head resting on her breast? Breathing thick, warm breath, arousing. Was it at the fridge she took off the watch? Tossed it on top, maybe? Or by the couch, at the window ledge. What did she say? "I don't want to wear this right now." Or was it "any more." "I'm taking it off. Umphff." She pulled it off with joyful abandon. I remember remarking on it. Momentarily considering how released she seemed, the watch unclasped. Off. I remember thinking how perhaps I should move it somewhere where it could be found easier later, but also thinking how the ledge, or wherever it was, seemed a perfectly safe place, and how I shouldn't interfere with people's actions, how, if she liked it there, wanted to leave it there, it was all right. Let it be. A couple days later, the email. In cryptic fashion, phrased like a want-ad for the newspaper, discreetly seeking a lost item. Promising a reward to an audience of one. The form of the email, an inside joke, made me laugh. But the reward part grabbed me. What exactly would be the currency of thanks? Leather or rubber accessories, gloves, boots, bodysuits, the vengeance of the furies, or graces of the triple moon goddess? I scanned the other emails she sent as well. Her "lost" electronic message arrived at my office in mid-morning. I wanted to go to the house right away and start looking. Wanted to throw off the office, leave it behind. Release myself. She said, "Just because we're doing this doesn't mean I'm leaving him." And of course I agreed. Transitions. Intersections. Ships passing on a mid-summer's night. A cliché, perhaps. Still, there was the matter of the lost time-piece. Lost in a moment when neither of us was fully attentive. Sucked down some warp-hole, or lying near the crumbling flanks of a half-formed memory. She got it from a close friend, her erst-while lover. Perhaps there was to be more with him. She hoped or meant for more, but somehow... time. Searching, I was conscious of the importance of not cre-ating a fiction of what had happened, conscious of the importance of not recreating the moment, for in that recreation there was bound to be distortion. Conscious of the need to suspend what I thought had happened and instead simply search without preconceptions as to the location of the thing. I knew if I projected onto memory, then it would metamorphose into a self-wrought story. The preconceived layers of events re-cre-ated would blur the actual. I had to suspend, stop time, thought. Wait for a period. At home, I searched the obvious places. Top of the fridge, window ledge near the couch, surrounding areas, between cushions on the couch, then the floor. The obvious places. I tried to suspend any internal dialogue, tried to see, remember what was there then, on the night of. Searched the second floor, bedrooms, closets, memory and slippage. Again, the window ledge, sheets, pillows, slip-cases, behind the couch in case it slid there, under, or onto the carpet. Blurs, slippage, new thoughts bumping into memories of the actual. Recalling motion, the porch, the slow dance of actions. Inside the house that night, she, wanting. Wanting me, inside. Aroused, drunk, outside of our heads, beyond the world's sticky grasp. Thinking hard. Mother-of-pearl. Smaller links. Spent. Her face in morning, obscured by locks, links of hair, pale features, sun, gold, the face clasped, calm, accented with open hands, nose-line almost aquiline, cool morning shadows accentuating cheekbones, lips, drawn, dawn, a photograph, discreetly sunlit through dim clouds, the city awakening, morning, a portrait, a series of photos stored in flawed memory, thinking of Stevens' blackbird, and his thirteen ways of looking, as I flip through moments layered, watching, seeking a watch that cannot be found. I could see, really see inside her, the distanced beauty, and when I spoke of it, she brushed me off with mock derision, then asked for more. Skin, supple, heart turning its gaze upon itself, deep gaze into, what was it? Later, she said,

"Just because I misplaced that watch doesn't mean…"
Twelve years. Her time. But no commitment. Nothing
ventured. Years lost, perhaps, but nothing truly lost…
except. She, thinking maybe marriage, with him, another. And then this, what? Passage or digression? And of all
times, the solstice. Diametrically opposed to the halcyon
days of winter. A magic equilibrium. A match struck.
Eyes illuminated by the candle's flickering. Fingering.
Books. Each other. Traces. Beautiful losers. Something
gained, maybe. Me, thinking, God is alive, Nietzsche is
dead, buried by latex kink fetish nurses in a freshly
turned plot. "I'm not really into the heavy bondage, ball-
gags that kind of thing," she says. "But sometimes, I like
the aesthetic." Research. And I'm listening, drinking her
words with red wine. And now, me, revisiting places in
time, unclasping temporal pockets that insisted themselves during the night when words gave shape to fists
raised previously in passion with smashed glasses, missed
appointments, opportunities. Her closeted places,
momentarily unlocked to reveal a coterie, half forgotten.
I listened, parched, perched, awaiting flight, restrained
and bound, awaiting release, a caged bird, singing words,
a command or permission, or ships, anchored adjacent
on the wine sea that brought us together. At port. No
fixed destination. Me departing marriage. After twelve
years. She considering one. Or not, the unspoken
thought. Uncovering old sores, bitter taste of each other's
pasts, inventing winter futures. Wine coaxing, tongue

fury, eyes on hands, loosened clothes, but still of two, maybe, three minds. Tongues freed, falling into each other's orbits, mouths, bodies. Later the morning. Then a couple days later, the email: "lost watch" and me searching mind and house, passing through that night again, bits at a time. Not knowing which to prefer, the beauty of inflection or the beauty of innuendo. I was relishing the pleasant anxiety of the task. But left wanting. "He gave me that watch." Thinking perhaps the loss or absence might somehow signify something of import. Innuendo. Sentimental value. An undefined inflection. The need to be on time for work, meetings, buses. Timing, a real need. And, now, me searching, and while searching, re-tracing our steps, movements. Hot breath on neck. Biting. Gentle. Or gentle-hard. Or hard. Her mouth, and mine. Wine and words. Touching. Crazy with night. We spoke paths. Opposite trajectories. But for the passing. Dancing. Predestination or free will. Veering. Comets accelerate when hurtling too close to planetary or stellar gravitational fields. "I'll never leave him." "Of course." And we both knew. And it was at this pocket of time, a closet where we hang umbrellas or coats, where we hesitated, came to a momentary standstill. I remember, here, time, breath, stopped for a period. It is little, but perhaps little enough, or more than enough. Thinking, there sometimes comes a moment when you hesitate, and say this isn't right, better withdraw, simplify, surrender to the confinement of words, and the lonely clasp of talk alone. But, there also comes a time when someone says, there can only be a single moment, brief as it is, in which passion rises, and on passing is gone forever, without return. And caution can't help. It needs to be fed or it will consume you instead, and to give in to caution, or to refuse to unlock the clasp is bondage, is to capitulate to the condition of absence unendurable, and to condone a hunger that renders the spirit too weak to sing for its breakfast. Abstinence and denial collide with tongue and thigh. Inflected innuendo arrested. Sometimes you must make the wrong choice, or you're dead, and you stay that way and know it. Sometimes it's best to leap without a parachute, into freefall, land on a couch, or bed, to taste hot summer in your mouth. Amidst the thunder and words, her aestive carnality reigned that night. And later, I found myself musing, recalling all this while searching for a time-piece. Thinking, maybe she still has it, always had it, but wants me to look, an arch dig, a playful card, knowing that as I'm looking, I'll be retracing the steps, here where we embraced, here when we first touched glasses filled red with wine, tracing, was it here, on the couch where we talked for what was it? Hours or seconds. Later, stars, the stairs, a room, and the window with ledges, a bed, where madness met delirium in the intoxicated night and sleep emerged as victor, where morning fingered her hair, her quiet shoulder, where dawn touched our lips awake. And so, I'm watching, searching, looking for a watch, but not finding it.

Wandering, bemused, wondering if maybe she still has it because I can't find it, or if she took it without thinking, or perhaps it will yet return or be returned, or one day be found in the bottom of a bag or drawer. And I'm thinking, perhaps the plumber, or electrician, or one of the maintenance people saw it, a day or so later. So many comings and goings, preparing the house, repairing it after my reasoned complaints to the landlord. Minor matters. The overhead light switch broken. The leaking tap. Broken locks on the window. Perhaps one of them noted the watch on the ledge, and without thinking put it safely aside, perhaps in one of my many cluttered drawers, or thinking swiftly, seized the purloined moment and stuffed it into a pocket. Our haste that morning did not enhance reflection, departing without breakfast. I'd gladly purchase a replacement. But there is the other matter of sentiment buried under temporal inflection, perhaps too personal an innuendo. Or, perhaps it will return at an unexpected moment stimulated by some liminal event, a tune on the radio, the turning of a card, or a page, and as I search the house, I pause momentarily at the inescapable rhythms of sleeping breath, rumpled sheets, morning, a sea washing through the window's glass, looking to the ledge for a watch that might've been there, is not there now, but if it was eyed and found, clasped in hand, passed to a second hand in an unbound moment, then time would stop

1.

URUZ

URUZ. THE OLD VÖLVA. Valandinne, is a seið-weaving cypher who writes in blood red runes under the pale moonlight. She lives alone in the rowan stand and sings galdr-healing spells. Odhinn's ravens Huginn and Muninn perch on her shoulders and end every incantation with a *"chok chok chok."*

Raido. Under a blue flax cloak Valandinne practises wortcunning and leechcraft. She keeps a magic black cat whose shadow stalking guides her into the Ginnunga-gap. She strums on a forked staff of yew. Every morning a spider weaves the rune ægishjálmr between the tines to bind the spell in the staff.

Ehwaz. And every night she rides her blue fjord horse Hrimfaxi into Hel where she stores stacks of shining runes.

Haglaz. *Qong!* Chimes the boiling cauldron and *aum* moans the Gjallrhorn...Valandinne transforms into a schillering blue star and sings the sampo in her staff. *Chymy*r. Valandinne tosses the runes onto the slopes of snow. *Clang*. Each rune is a gleaming door into a time closet.

Dagaz. The tinkling icicles fall into a crystal goblet of Kvasir's blood. Valandinne, pouring it, cleanses the doors of perception.

2.

HAGLAZ

Valandinne the Renegade invites you to howl the galdr spell of Lifthrasir★

Uruz Uruz Uruz
The world I am dreaming is the world I am living now
My ancestors are beside me
I sing the ones who sing me
The golden cock crows Ragnarok
And I must hold fast to my heart
And not let it wander into the Hel of night
Stones take flight
And the bloody crescent moon bites the celestial sky
The old gods are burning in dragonfire
And life is only a matter of time for
the two hearts the Horn of Heimdallr is a harbinger of
doom
But I am Lifthrasir of one heart
And Gjallr is a herald of victory
Haglaz Haglaz Haglaz
And out of the holocaust I will come flying
High on the wings of the eagle
I will witness the greening of the earth
Raido Raido Raido
The new runes will fall golden into the grasses
For Valandinne will break the locked doors of perception
And fling open the closets of time.
Wunjo Wunjo Wunjo

3

RAIDO

My name is Valandinne the seeress. And I record my memories of the past and of the future in blood bound books. For I am the spæ-kona who practices the seið and the living memories of these sagas must not be forgotten. Every year I, Valandinne of Vidolf, am re-born in the spindle whorl of the four winds. I am Valandinne of Svarthofdi and if you have forgotten the old charms I will remember them for you.

For the raven Muninn is our past and our future, and the raven Huginn is our present thought.

When the stones move, they move with passion, and when the trees whisper on the wind, the wings of black birds carry the message to us. The old woman holds the keys to the kingdom of heaven and lives among us, as grandmother, mother, sister, wife, daughter. I, Valandinne, wyrd sister of the woods, have written the runes on my staff to remind you that all of life is sacred. I, Valandinne Vindalf, wind staff, blow away the illusion of time with my seið Vardðlokur. *Remember.* When I come from the south I am the yellow jaguar of the hot roar and when I come from the west I am the black wind of the raining raven and when I come from the north I am the snow-white Wolverine wind of victory over fire and when I come from the east I am the red bear of remembrance. In thecentre of the four winds it is only me Valandinne, your Grandmother shaman.

Remember me and don't be afraid. I am only shapeshifting into the green-eyed jet-black cat to seek out the spell of illusion that binds you to time.

For I, Valandinne völva, do solemnly swear to reveal the runes of Urðr, *what is happening*, Verðandi, *what is beginning to happen,* and Skuld, *what will rightly happen.* So that when the tides of time flow backwards, all who heed the prophecies of the seið-kona will remember their future-past. And walk backwards into their closets to retrieve the mementos they have saved to survive in the next world.

4.

WUNJO

Bring me your amulets of golden Amber
Bring me the red and black raven banner
Bring me your babes both girl and boy
And I will bless them with the rune of joy

All from old Norse traditions

*völva, staff wielding seeress
*seið-kona female practitioner of shaman magic
*Lifthrasir, the person who lives through the end of the world or
  Ragnarok
*spæ-kona, spa-wife—one who knows the *Ørlög* or ancient law
*Urðr, Verðandi, Skuld, The Norns or the Three Fates.

RICHARD TRUHLAR

OPENING THE CLOSET DOOR and forgetting, forgetting what's in the closet, what's been left in the closet, what's been in the closet for some time, time having a way of providing forgetfulness—except for remembering the one thing that you're needing to extract, to bring into the open and remember again, make it part of the present—you crouch down and peer in.

The present of the closet, however, is darkling as your hand begins to grope around among the containers and boxes, the contours of which you are familiar with but the contents of which remain speculative—*When was the last time I was in the closet?*

The last time, you remember, was... it was when you last wrote something (everything he writes is always put in the closet, stored there amongst the various collectibles, souvenirs, scrapbooks, photo albums—so that prying eyes or curious minds would see only a detritus of objects as if a rock facing had, over time, crumbled and fallen on to the closet floor, guaranteeing that any intruder would be discouraged from making any order or sense from it), but you can't remember exactly where you hid your writing book.

You grope, your hands moving over shapes indistinct or unseen, finding at last the box you feel must house your quest—haul it out on to your bedroom floor—open the lid.

The various items contained within are piled upon one another—a gas mask from a war long ago, a crudely carved statue of some deity given to you by an elderly neighbour who had traversed jungles, a switchblade knife, and beneath these lay the skull of a cat, yellowed with age, the teeth like ivory, sharper than you would have expected.

(He remembers the hot summer day, how bored he was, how alone, walking the road in front of his home, suddenly spotting the black clump by the curb, advancing until he recognized the roadkill, the small breathless cat, motionless and surrounded by buzzing flies—how he ran back to his house, retrieved a paper bag, put the small body into it, carried it up a hill that the new housing division had not yet encroached upon, found a suitable place and dug a hole, buried it, a ritual—and some time after, his memory of it mutating into curiosity, he dug it up, the body now fleshless but hair still present, retrieving the skull, his trophy which he took back to his bedroom and placed on his desk—the next day, getting up in the morning, discovering the maggots crawling from the eye and nose apertures.)

§

Having sat at my writing desk for the past hour, conjuring that memory of childhood, creating six paragraphs signifying a private conversation between my selves, I stretch and get up, move into the adjacent kitchen, open the refrigerator door to get a drink.

I notice that their bowls are empty and refill them, then open the back porch door, call out, and they come in, all three of them—one completely jet black, the other two like a calico of black and white patterning—their eyes green and yellow jewels. They eat together, drink from the same water bowl, occasionally looking behind them to where I stand watching them, and then when I move they move with me, following me, pretending to not acknowledge me but padding soundlessly beside my feet. Wherever I go in the house, they circumscribe me, their eyes never fully upon me, never staring, just glancing in order to manoeuvre according to my movements, and I feel helpless to rid myself of them.

They are three. I am one.

§

"...a past of increasing density drowns the sound of his present words..."

§

Sweating...it's a hot night...no air moving in the room and you lying on your bed in what feels like a puddle, sensations crawling over your skin so that you are scratching at phantom itches on your body, your mind crawling with images of your past, your present, your dread of the future...

You get up, look out your bedroom window; the trees are starkly still, the back-yard garden steaming in the humidity, your ears picking out almost inaudible chitter-ings, flutterings, muffled cries—you move back to bed, lie down, gradually move in and out of a restless sleep, all the while imagining your garden in the night where insectoid forms slowly creep along soil, creep up the walls of your house, creep through cracks and creep through holes, move noiselessly across walls and floors—legs, hundreds of legs, chitinous legs...

...and it's then you hear them, not legs, not footfalls, but floorboards, the hardwood floorboards outside your bedroom door creaking, creaking in the way that only floorboards can creak when they are weighted by stepping, a stepping itself a silence to the human ear but which in its weight signals the floorboards to creak, and you know that the creaking is a stepping even though you can't hear the stepping, and you know that the creaking that is a stepping is a pacing, a pacing back and forth on the other side of your bedroom door, and the creaking is polyrhythmic, is a trio of unheard stepping.

§

Remember that time? You do, don't you—a door opening downstairs, people's voices loud with pain, with confusion—you hearing an animal's screams, footsteps running upstairs... you jumped from your near-sleep up from your bed, rushed out your bedroom door, saw your family standing at your younger son's room door, yourself rushing to it, looking into the room.

There he was, a calico of black and white patterning, on a chair, a sound you had never heard issuing from his mouth, tail missing, half a paw gone, blood across the floor, dripping from the chair ledge. You moved towards him, speaking words he could never understand, hoping the tone of your voice would comfort him, and it was then the scream ripped the air as his teeth bit into his wounds, trying to bite away the pain in a frenzy, to bite away reality...you never forgetting.

§

A small boy opens a closet door, looking to find his writing book, his head full of fictions. What possibly could he find?

AFTERWORDS

WHEREVER I GO, WHEN away from home, I always have a notebook with me so that I can capture phrases or ideas which I'll possibly use later in my fiction or poetry. One such phrase came to me on a streetcar on my way home from work—"the closets of time"—and it resonated with what I was reading—the works of H.P. Lovecraft. The phrase stayed with me for the rest of the day, until late evening, when it gave birth to the idea behind this anthology.

What would happen, I thought to myself, if I invited a group of writers to each create a short fiction entitled "The Closets of Time"? The works then would be assembled into an anthology entitled *The Closets of Time*, but the individual works would, of necessity, not be individually titled within the book. The interest and excitement for myself was in how each writer would manifest the ideas of "closets" and "time" in his or her writing, and what kind of echoes or resonances would be evident across all the works.

I also felt that I wanted the anthology to span genres, from speculative fiction to experimental work to surrealism, for instance; I wanted imaginative writers, mature writers who felt comfortable taking risks with their writing, dangerous perhaps in their language and structure. So I made up an initial list of those writers whom I both admired and felt could create *The Closets of Time*, and approached Beverley Daurio at The Mercury Press with the idea, to see if she might like to co-edit the book. Excited by the idea, we set to work, brainstorming and adding to the list of writers. I began by creating a description of the proposed book and what was looked for, and set to soliciting work for the anthology.

Invitations to contribute went out, to writers in Canada and the United States, some of whom I knew, and some total strangers. The seventeen writers herein took up the challenge of creating a new work specifically for this book; and together they have formed *The Closets of Time*.

Dreams, memories, myths, and fables are in evidence in *The Closets of Time*, and enclosed spaces, both mental and physical, constitute the walls of *The Closets of Time*. If you peer into *The Closets of Time*, you may see a machine to save you from tragedy, or spy a postcard from an old childhood neighbourhood. If you venture further in, you'll meet The Man with the Borrowed Organs and the

Norns. And if you rummage through the various boxes in *The Closets of Time*, you'll find this very book. I hope you enjoyed it.

Richard Truhlar

MOST LITERARY BOOKS begin with a writer's idea and long, singular work. Manuscripts are completed by their authors, and then submitted. Though some books begin with their publishers, the process, whether manuscripts are solicited or arrive over the transom, is usually one of vetting and selecting from available manuscripts.

Anthologies, on the other hand, though they also begin with ideas and parameters—from editors, writers, or other folk with a collectivity in mind—most often start with a book in potential that already exists in scattered form, asking to be gathered and organized. Anthologies also often seek to answer questions: what is going on in contemporary Canadian poetry, for example; or what are green theorists considering in terms of ecological solutions; or who are the current experimental writers of fiction, and what kind of fiction is that at this moment in Canada?

Anthologies can be fascinating creatures to watch as they form, sometimes surprising, sometimes nudging edges of the ideas with which the editor began into new shapes. Starting from scratch with *The Closets of Time*, Richard Truhlar's idea of inviting writers to create new short fictions under the title "The Closets of Time," was an immediately engaging one. I was especially curious about how fiction is in motion in 2007, how the metaphysics and tangibleness of the title would become manifest in these writers' work, and about the form the book would take once compiled.

The fictions for *Closets* were written over an approximately three-month period during the summer of 2007. A delicate tapestry of styles, imagery, and concerns emerged—the psychology of economics, linens redolent of lavender, forests looming above small human actions, a slow rush to an appointment, cliffs of self-knowledge, ancient Norse runes, a contemporary Frankenstein, surrealist shopping carts, a watch as trope in an erotic affair, secret boxes of hidden writings...

As Richard and I discussed methods of ordering the book, grumping a bit at the thought of alphabetizing by name, or working from chronology or place, Richard suggested a "mirror canon"—a musical term referring to sections of a piece balancing each other outward from the centre—and we began to organize the pieces we considered resonant with each other, placing them opposite one another in the text. Also considered were the resonances between works—and it felt to to us as if the elements fell into aesthetic place. The hope is that the contributors, and readers, agree.

The process of making *The Closets of Time* into a book, from working with writers and texts to page design, was a pleasurable experience. And reading and editing the book has been like a strange, joyful, seventeen-course meal: from the delicacy of hard doors opening in the dark, to sensual walks through unknown cities, liberating R&B music, new faces flying in through windows, to the philosophy of invisible text, a protective, unmerciful mother, and a painted young man surrounded by birds.

Replete with unexpected delights.

Beverley Daurio

EDITORS' ACKNOWLEDGEMENTS

I want to thank Beverley Daurio for her commitment to and hard work on this anthology; Misha Nogha for her generous advice; and the contributors who together have created this book.

Richard Truhlar

Thanks to my fellow editor, Richard Truhlar, for many bright day patios, serious work in fraternity, and consultation; to Gordon Robertson, for the cover design; and to the writers in this book for leaping into the unknown with us.

Beverley Daurio

AUTHOR BIOGRAPHIES

Gary Barwin is a writer, composer, and performer. He is the author of numerous books and chapbooks of poetry and fiction including the poetry collections *frogments from the frag pool: haiku after basho* (written with derek beaulieu), *Raising Eyebrows* and *Outside the Hat* (Coach House Books) and the fiction collections *Doctor Weep and other strange teeth*, *Big Red Baby* (The Mercury Press) and *Cruelty to Fabulous Animals* (Moonstone Press). You can visit Gary's website at: <www.garybarwin.com>.

Melody Sumner Carnahan has six books in print and numerous short works published in magazines and anthologies. She has worked with composers and performers for two decades to present her writing off the page, including live "performance novels," soundtracks for film and video, and in recordings from Tellus, NonesuchElectra, 4-Tay Records, Frog Peak Music, HighMayhem.org., and on Morton Subotnick's DVD-CD-rom *Gestures* (Mode Records, 2001). She lives in New Mexico and is a founding editor of Burning Books. You can visit Melody's website at: <http://www.burningbooks.org/>.

Beverley Daurio is the editor of *Dream Elevators: Interviews with Canadian Poets, The Power to Bend Spoons: Interviews with Canadian Novelists*, and of several anthologies of new fiction, including *Sex: An Anthology, Vivid: Stories by Five Women, Love & Hunger: New Fiction,* and *Hard Times.* Her fiction has been published in Canada, Australia, England, Romania, and the US. She is the author of several books and chapbooks, including *Hell & Other Novels* (Coach House/Talon) and lives in Toronto.

Michael Dean is a writer living in Toronto. He has been a sound poet and performance artist, having performed in Europe and across Canada. He is the author of *In Search of the Perfect Lawn*, and *The Walled Garden*, both published by Black Moss Press. For more information please contact Michael at <indian.trail@sympatico.ca>.

Brian Dedora leads a precise life in Vancouver working in his gilding studio laying, like craft cheese slices, leaves of gold, while expanding his Canadian abstract art collection and writing about it when he's not out sailing. Born in Vernon, B.C., in 1946, he received his B.A. from the University of Victoria in 1970. A founding editor of Underwhich Editions, he is a writer and performance artist whose work has been anthologized and widely published in special and limited editions. He is the author of *White Light* and *With WK in the Workshop: A Memoir of William Kurelek* (both The Mercury Press).

Paul Dutton is a poet, fictioneer, essayist, musician and former member of the Four Horsemen poetry-performance group. Born in Toronto where he continues to live, he is the author of several books, including *Visionary Portraits* (The Mercury Press), *Right Hemisphere Left Ear* (Coach House Press), *The Book of Numbers* (Porcupine's Quill), *The Plastic Typewriter* (Underwhich Editions) and *Aurealities* (Coach House Press). His first novel is *Several Women Dancing* (The Mercury Press).

Brian Evenson is the Director of the Literary Arts Program at Brown University. He is the author of seven books of fiction, most recently *The Open Curtain* and *The Wavering Knife* (which won the IHG Award for best story collection). He has translated work by Christian Gailly, Jean Frémon and Jacques Jouet. He has received an O. Henry Prize as well as an NEA fellowship. You can visit Brian's website at: <www.brianevenson.com>.

Karl Jirgens is the author of *A Measure of Time* (The Mercury Press) and *Strappado: Elemental Tales* (Coach House Press). His essays and fiction have appeared in *Open Letter*, *Impulse*, *Descant*, *Books in Canada* and many other venues. He is the founder of *Rampike Magazine*, which he edited from 1979 to 1994, and a former editorial board member of Underwhich Editions.

Lesley McAllister's travel writing has appeared in *The Globe and Mail* and *NOW Magazine*. Author of *The Blue House*, her essay "Ponds of Parkdale" was broadcast on CBC Radio. From 1981-84, she was the editor and publisher of *Identity*, a series of literary/visual chapbooks. She lives in Toronto where, among other things, she reviews mysteries.

Misha Nogha is the author of *Red Spider White Web*, *Kequa-hawkas*, and *Prayers of Steel*. She has just completed two new works, a novel of magic realism, *Yellowjacket*; and *Magpies & Tigers*, a collection of poetry and prose, published by Wordcraft of Oregon in July, 2007. Misha is the SkyWarn Severe Storm Spotter for NOAA and a Co-op Observer for the National Weather Service, and she raises Norwegian Fjord horses at Badger Sett Farm in Cove, Oregon. You can visit Misha's website at: <www.mishanogha.com>.

Lance Olsen is author of eight novels, one hypertext, four critical studies, four short-story collections, a poetry chapbook, and a textbook about fiction writing, as well as editor of two collections of essays about innovative contemporary fiction. His short stories, essays, poems, and reviews have appeared in hundreds of journals, magazines, and anthologies, including *Fiction International, Iowa Review,*

Village Voice, Time Out, BOMB, Gulf Coast, and *Best American Non-Required Reading.* He and his wife, assemblage-artist Andi Olsen, divide their time between the mountains of central Idaho and Salt Lake City, where he teaches at the University of Utah. You can visit Lance's website at: <www.lanceolsen.com>.

John Riddell's first published story appeared in 1963 and his work continued to appear in little magazines like *Kontakte, Ganglia, Descant* and *grOnk.* An early associate of *Ganglia* magazine, he later became a contributing editor of *grOnk* and then, in 1975, co-founded Phenomenon Press with Richard Truhlar. He has had visual work in exhibitions in Europe and Canada and his published books include *How to Grow Your Own Lightbulbs* and *Transitions* (Mercury), *a/z does it* (Nightwood Editions), *Criss-Cross* (Coach House Press), and *E clips E* (Underwhich Editions).

Stuart Ross, author of many books, including *Henry Kafka,* and *The Mud Game* (with Gary Barwin), is a notorious small-press activist and performer. He is the editor of *Mondo Hunkamooga: a journal of small press stuff, Surreal Estate: 13 Canadian Poets under the Influence,* and he fronts the trio Pod Squad. He has sold over 7,000 copies of his fiction and poetry on the streets of Toronto and is co-founder of the Toronto Small Press Book Fair. You can visit Stuart's website at: <www.hunkamooga.com>.

John Shirley is the author of numerous books and many, many short stories. His novels include *Crawlers, Demons, In Darkness Waiting*, and seminal cyberpunk works *City Come A-Walkin'* and the *A Song Called Youth* trilogy. His collections include the Bram Stoker and International Horror Guild award-winning *Black Butterflies* and *Really Really Really Really Weird Stories*. He also writes for screen (*The Crow*) and television. As a musician Shirley has fronted his own bands and written lyrics for Blue Oyster Cult and others. You can visit the authorized fan site at: <www.dark-echo.com/JohnShirley>.

Steven Ross Smith writes poetry, prose and explores the realms of sound and performance poetry. He has published, by performance or in print, in England, Holland, Russia, Portugal, the US, and Canada. His twelve published books include, among others, *Ritual Murders* (Turnstone Press), *Blind Zone* (Aya Press), *Lures,* and *Transient Light* (The Mercury Press) and four books in his poetic *fluttertongue* series, with Thistledown, Hagios, Turnstone and NeWest presses, respectively. He is a founding editor of Underwhich Editions and is the Executive Director of Sage Hill Writing Experience. You can visit Steven's website at: <www.fluttertongue.ca>.

Lola Lemire Tostevin has published seven collections of poetry, including *Site-Specific Poems* (Mercury). She has also published two novels, *Frog Moon* (Cormorant) and *Jasmine Man* (KeyPorter), and one collection of critical essays, *Subject to Criticism* (Mercury).

Richard Truhlar is a poet, fictioneer and text/sound/ musical composer. He has had seven books of his literary works published: *The Hollow and other fictions, A Porcelain Cup Placed There, Utensile Paradise, Figures in Paper Time, Parisian Novels, The Pitch,* and *Dynamite in the Lung.* As a performer, he was a member of the progressive new wave band Warm Jets, of the sound–poetry quartet Owen Sound, and of the electroacoustic chamber ensemble Tekst. You can visit Richard's website at: <www.richardtruhlar.com>.

Marquis Book Printing Inc.

Québec, Canada
2007